A murdered female impersonator caught with her skirt up...
Seattle's most exclusive gay cabaret...
love and deceit...
a suave and patient spider...
the tangled web we weave...
a missing 12th century Saracen dagger...
dungeons and secret passages...
a butler in the wings...
missing fingers and diamond rings...
hinky hoodlums and star-crossed lovers...
what money can't buy...
bent genders on a twisted street...
racy photographs...
mirrors and illusions...
near-naked nymphs...
big game hunters...
J. Edgar Hoover...
fighting Commies and other undesirables...
blackmail and payoffs...
flying fists and velvet gloves...
hypocrites and heroes...
too much—too soon—too late...
the third degree...
coming clean...
and ain't love strange?

Jake Rossiter
A Seattle private detective who's been through so many
hard knocks that he calls his hometown Rat City

Miss Jenkins
Rossiter's ex-girl Friday, now private eye partner, who's
ready for more action than Jake anticipates

Stanley "Heine" Heinselman
Rossiter's ex-Marine war buddy and best pal—
the Rossiter Detective Agency's main operative

Manny Velcker
The handsome, sharp, and natty veteran op of the
Rossiter Detective Agency

Lieutenant Baker
A veteran Seattle homicide detective, a straight-shooter,
and the only cop Rossiter trusts

Marty Haggerty
Rossiter's longtime big-game hunting attorney

Trixie
A part-time cabana boy and up-and-coming
female impersonator at the Garden of Allah

Chuck Osbourne
The assistant manager of the Camlin Hotel,
who moonlights as Trixie's "manager"

Royce Bennington
Suave, jaded, fabulously wealthy, and used to getting what
he wants anytime and anyhow

Donny
The rich, elevator-shoe-wearing co-owner of
the gay cabaret, the Garden of Allah

Martin
Donny's dirt-poor partner in life, as well as in
the Garden of Allah

Rollo Mudd
One of Seattle's most powerful gangsters, always seen
with his trademark brown bowler hat

Dennis Diamond
Rollo Mudd's main muscle and best-boy

Abe & Lorna Horowitz
The cuckolded husband & the young, cheating wife

Judge Torrence
A federal judge who walks an increasingly narrow line

Also by Curt Colbert

Rat City

Sayonaraville

Queer Street

Curt Colbert

UglyTown
Los Angeles

First Edition

UGLYTOWN AND THE UGLYTOWN COIN LOGO SERVICEMARK REG. U.S. PAT. OFF.

Library of Congress Cataloging-in-Publication Data data on file.
ISBN: 0-9724412-9-8
ISBN (Limited Ed.): 0-9758503-4-2

Find out more of the mystery: UglyTown.com/QueerStreet

Printed in the United States of America

10 9 8 7 6 5 4 3 2 1

in memory of Skippy LaRue

Queer Street

Chapter

1

I WAS JUST HAVING A PRIVATE CHUCKLE
with Miss Jenkins when the phone rang.

"Don't answer it," she ordered.

"Got to, doll," I said, crossing over to my desk. "It's probably Heine. He's supposed to let me know where to meet him tomorrow night."

"Oh, fudge," she muttered, as I picked up the receiver.

"Hey, Heine."

"No, it's me, Martin! You've got to get down here right away!"

"Martin?" I asked, trying to get my bearings.

Miss Jenkins gave me an odd look.

"Look, Martin, I've got a dinner date and it's—"

"But it's murder!" he yelled.

"—my birthday … " I paused. "What'd you say?"

"Murder! There's been a murder!"

"Yeah? Who got killed?"

"Trixie," he said, with a gasp. "Poor Trixie. Here at the club. You've got to help!"

"Slow down," I told him, grabbing a Philip Morris. "Who's Trixie?"

"One of our female impersonators. She's the best." He

began to sob. "We found her stabbed in her dressing room backstage. Oh, God."

"Take it easy." I fired up my smoke. "You know who did it?"

"No."

"You call the cops?"

"Can't."

"Look, Martin—"

"We'll pay you whatever you want."

"That's not the point."

"Come as quick as you can! Please."

The line went dead.

I cradled the receiver and glanced across the desk at Miss Jenkins, who had taken a seat in the wingback chair opposite me. She looked stunning in her forest green cocktail dress, cut surprisingly low, which probably cost her a month's pay. Her stiletto heels added a good three inches to her height, making her as leggy as any of the glamour queens in the latest fashion mags.

I was about to break the bad news to her, when she chimed in first.

"Save it," she told me. "I heard you on the phone. There's been some stupid murder somewhere, and we're not going out for your birthday dinner."

"Of course we are, kid," I said, checking the .45 in my shoulder holster and grabbing my overcoat and fedora from the coat tree by my desk. "We can't have you all dressed up with no place to go. We'll just make a quick detour, that's all."

"Sure," she said, following me out through the office. "Sure."

Miss Jenkins didn't say another word until we got outside, where her '48 Plymouth coupe sat waiting at the curb.

Freshly washed and waxed, it glistened in the light from the nearby street lamp and looked just as new as it had on the showroom floor last year.

Miss Jenkins insisted on driving. Still sulking as I slid into the front seat beside her, she put the key into the ignition, then paused and asked, "Where are we going, anyway?"

Martin was the co-owner of the Garden of Allah, which was located on First Avenue below Union Street, about two miles south of our office in the Denny Regrade. It was one of those clubs that wasn't supposed to exist in Seattle. Or most anywhere else, for that matter.

"You mean there's illegal gambling there, or something like that?" asked Miss Jenkins as we cruised south down First Avenue. "Bookmaking, maybe? Prostitution? Drugs?"

Pressed on a concise definition of just what made the Garden of Allah so hinky, I said, "Let's put it this way, Miss Jenkins: it's the type of joint where men dance with men, and women dance with women—if you get my drift."

"Say, how do you know about this place? Don't tell me you've been there before."

"Only in an official capacity, my dear. I did a little favor for the owners back before you came aboard," I said, as Miss Jenkins began to break the speed limit. "O.K., watch your driving. I want to get there in one piece."

She gave me one of her looks and pushed the gas pedal even harder. As the telephone poles whizzed by faster and faster, she said, "At least tell me who got murdered. Who was it?"

"Some joe named Trixie. One of their female impersonators."

"Female impersonator? A man who dresses up like a woman?"

"That's what I said."

"No kidding? Gee whiz, I've never seen one of them."

"Well, you're about to. That's it coming up at the end of the block. Pull over near the corner."

She did as ordered, sliding up to the curb like she drove: fast and slick.

The street in front of the joint was pretty quiet, very few people or cars going by, as most of Seattle's movie theatres and dance clubs were farther east, away from the dives on seamy First Avenue. I was glad of that, since I really didn't want anybody to see me traipsing into the Garden of Allah. As we bailed out of Miss Jenkins's Plymouth, I noted that there weren't any police cruisers in sight.

Miss Jenkins noticed too. "Why aren't there any cops here?" she asked, tying her floral print scarf tightly under her chin against the late March breeze.

"Called us first," I told her. "Keeping it under wraps until we've had a look-see."

"Where is this club, anyway?" she asked, giving the buildings on our side of the street a hard look. "I don't see anything but some old buildings and that tavern."

"They don't exactly advertise, Miss Jenkins. It's down in the tavern's basement."

The tavern was called the Sailor Boy. Connected to a turn-of-the-century, red brick hotel, it was as nondescript as rough-and-tumble First Avenue, which got progressively worse as you followed it south into Pioneer Square's skid road area. The lights were on, but you couldn't see inside because its eight-foot-tall, peeling, wood-framed windows were blacked out up to a height of about six feet. Miss Jenkins glued an eyeball to the windows, trying to sneak a peek anyway, until I pulled her under the marble archway

that led to the foyer that the Sailor Boy shared with the adjoining Arlington Hotel.

"I wanted to see what was going on," she complained.

"You'll be seeing more than your share," I told her, pulling open the old oak & brass trimmed door.

Once inside the little foyer, you could go left into the tavern, whose juke was loudly kicking out the latest Sinatra tune, or right into the hotel's main hallway, or continue just past the tavern door to a narrow stairwell, above which a small, stenciled sign read, THE GARDEN OF ALLAH—PRIVATE CLUB, complete with a red arrow that pointed down the stairs.

"Ladies first," I said, gesturing down the stairwell with a sweeping flourish.

Miss Jenkins hesitated. In the end, though, her natural curiosity won out, and she scampered down the stairs so fast that I had to hurry to catch up. When I reached her side, she was just taking off her scarf and admiring the wide, white French doors that led into the club.

"Those are lovely," she said. "I've always wanted French doors. Don't you like the way they've done the sheers on the inside of them?" she asked, referring to the lemon-yellow draperies that partially obscured the view inside the club.

"Very chic. A lot nicer than its old days as a speakeasy," I told her. Then I rang the little brass-plated buzzer beside the entrance. From the sound of voices and laughter that could be heard, it seemed like the Garden of Allah was still as full of patrons as most any night, which was strange considering that a murder had just taken place.

The drapes parted ever so slightly—just enough for somebody to give us a quick eyeball from the other side—then the door opened right up for us. It was Martin himself acting as doorman. I hadn't seen him since Big Ed's funeral a few years back, but he hadn't changed much—tall and lanky, just a little rough around the edges, he looked like he'd be more comfortable in denims and a work shirt rather than the tuxedo he wore. Late forties and clean shaven, he always reminded me of Gary Cooper except for his high-pitched voice.

"Jake! I'm so glad you came. Come in, come in," he said.

While Martin closed and locked the door after us, I surveyed the joint. It had changed very little. At first glance, the Garden of Allah was like a hundred other clubs around town. A decent sized dance floor, ringed by about forty white linen-covered tables, each with a crystal bud vase holding a single red rose. Coat check was next to the main entrance. A podium for the maître d'. A long, curved, open bar, fronted by a dozen upholstered stools to the right. A gleaming white Wurlitzer electric organ beside the stage. The decorating scheme ran to lemon-yellow and lime green silks and satins. Other than that, it seemed as normal as any other club you might hit in the wee hours.

"So, Martin," I said, taking off my fedora, "what's the skinny? Where's the stiff?"

"I'll show you in a little bit." He took my hat and managed a weak smile. "I'm short staffed and everything's in a fluster. I'll get you a table."

"Table? We don't want a table," I said, noticing that Miss Jenkins's jaw had dropped clear to her knees as she perused the scene inside the club: it was everything I'd told her about, males with males, likewise with the few females, and included some couples whose gender I couldn't quite figure out.

"I've got a nice table right up by the dance floor." Martin took off toward the front of the club, not leaving us much choice but to follow him.

"Golly," whispered Miss Jenkins, as we wove our way between the crowded tables. "This place is strange."

Martin pulled chairs out for us at a table near the organ.

"Thanks," said Miss Jenkins, sliding into her seat.

I didn't sit. "We don't need a table," I told Martin. "Besides—"

"Sit, sit," he said. "I have to go find Donny." He turned and quickly strode backstage.

"Hey," I called after him.

"Oh, sit down, Jake," Miss Jenkins told me. "It won't hurt to wait a few minutes."

"I don't like being jacked around," I said. "Anyway, what about our dinner? You were sure in an all-fired hurry before Martin called to get us down here."

"We've got half an hour or so." She grabbed my wrist and pulled me down into my seat. Then her eyes darted around the club, a trace of a smile forming on her lips as she continued. "Besides, I've never been in a place like this. It's really kind of fascinating."

"It'll wear off."

"So, how *do* you know about this place?"

"It was perfectly innocent, Miss Jenkins."

"Sure."

"You want the story or not?"

She bit her tongue and nodded *yes*.

"It was after Heine and I got home from the Pacific. We were out celebrating. We'd painted the town red from one end to the other until all the bars closed. Like I said, this place used to be a speakeasy I frequented. That's why I thought of it. It was the only joint still open downtown."

"They let you in?" she asked.

"Yeah. What'd I just say?"

"Hmmnn, they must have thought you were together."

"Ha-ha. Anyway, we didn't know what kind of a place it had turned into. All we knew was they were still serving and we were still thirsty. Well, we went to check our coats and saw two big thugs just beating the hell out of this short, stocky joe in the coatroom behind the counter. They were working him over pretty bad."

"What did you do?"

"What do you think? We never liked two-on-one, so we jumped in and evened the odds. Heine introduced one tough to his blackjack, and I introduced the other to a left-hook and a solid right-cross. Turned out they were collectors for a local gangster. The little guy they'd been hammering was none other than Donny, Martin's partner. He was grateful as could be. Offered us free drinks for the rest of the night, but we declined, owing to the nature of the joint, and blew out to one of the after-hours jazz clubs up on Jackson Street. Anyway, Donny and Martin steered a couple cases with heavy moola our way over the next few years to show their gratitude. And that brings us to today. End of story."

Just then, this tall, knockout dame wearing a tight silver lame gown, complete with a flaming pink feathered boa, came out from the stage door, followed by a short, redheaded joe in a blue serge suit. The crowd applauded mightily when they saw them. I expected somebody to come out and MC their act. But that wasn't the case. Instead, they simply took a bow, and launched right into their gig. The little guy hopped up onto the big, white Wurlitzer's organ bench and began to play, as the dame stepped behind the silver microphone by the organ and started to sing her heart out. Her low, sultry voice perfectly matched the tune she warbled: "Begin the Beguine."

"Say, she's really good," said Miss Jenkins.

"That's a man," I told her.

"No!"

"Yes, it is."

She leaned across the table, peering so hard at the gorgeous songbird that I thought she'd end up with permanent crow's feet. "Can't be ... " she muttered. "Anyway, how would you know?"

"Trust me; I just know," I said, firing up a smoke and thinking, for a brief moment, that it was too bad the singer wasn't a dame: she was a real looker.

"Well," Miss Jenkins said, sitting up straight again. "I beg to differ. I know a woman when I see one. She's got cleavage for Heaven's sake. That's definitely a woman."

"Where the hell is Martin?" I said, taking a quick gander around the club. "This is getting ridiculous. You stay here. I'm going to go find him."

I got up and went backstage through the door that Martin had used. It was a much bigger area than I'd expected, and soon found myself in a dim hallway that came to a T. The corridor to the right was pitch black, none of the overhead bulbs working, so I went to the left. About twenty feet down, I came to a door marked, DRESSING ROOM. I didn't bother knocking, just went right in and got a surprise: an eyeful of two young joes in their skivvies—nothing I hadn't seen before, but the slimmer of the two was dressed in women's underwear, complete with nylons and garter belt, and was in the process of being cinched tightly into a stiff corset by his pal. "God, I can't believe they expect me to get ready in ten minutes," he was saying. "It usually takes me an hour to get into my—" He broke off when he saw me. "Hey," he told me. "Don't you ever bother knocking?"

"Guess not," I said, thinking his get-up looked pretty strange with his short crew cut.

"No customers allowed back here, mister," the other one told me, tying off the corset, which had squeezed his buddy's waist into a perfect hourglass shape.

"Maybe we can make an exception," said the crew cut joe, turning fully to face me, hands on his hips, and a smile forming on his lips. "He's kind of rugged."

"I'm looking for Martin. He came back this way. You seen him?"

The other one shrugged, then told me, "Try down the hall. This isn't the only dressing room, you know."

"Hope you stick around for my act," said the crew cut joe, adjusting the fasteners to his garter belt.

I answered by leaving—continued up the hallway, where I found two more dressing rooms. The first was empty. The second contained a corpse.

She was sprawled on her back in the middle of the floor, her blonde hair a mess, and her red evening gown rumpled halfway up her shapely legs. As I got closer, I saw that the lovely dame was really a man. The blonde hair was a wig, and what I'd taken for dark red polka dots were bloodstains that had seeped through the bright red gown.

It looked like a struggle had taken place. The floor was strewn with various makeup, and the mirror over the dressing table at the back of the room had blood spatters on it. The blood formed a trail right up to the body.

I was just going over to give things a thorough check, when I got rudely interrupted.

Two cops, guns drawn, burst into the dressing room.

"Hands up!" they yelled. "You're under arrest!"

Chapter

2

NORMALLY, SPENDING A FEW HOURS IN THE pokey isn't all that bad. It can give you time to think, even relax a little, as long as you know that you'll get bailed out shortly and won't have any problem setting things straight once you hit the street again.

Such should have been the case this evening. I definitely hadn't done anything wrong. The idiot cops would soon find that I held a valid private dick license. And I could count on the fact that Miss Jenkins would have Haggerty, my lawyer, quickly posting bail and getting me sprung. So, why wasn't I just taking five on my bunk and enjoying a smoke or two?

The answer was painfully simple: damned flatfeet that collared me had spread the story about where I'd been picked up and the kind of company I was keeping. None of the cops had said anything directly to me, yet, but they'd been giving me a lot of odd looks. It wasn't a good situation. But, I'd learned a long time ago, that bad as things could get, there was always something worse. In this case, that was two burly cops bringing me a cellmate: Martin, all beat up and squawking like a chicken bound for the stewpot.

"Maybe you'll feel more talkative after you spend some time in here," said the heavier of the two cops as they tossed

Martin in with me. He landed smack on his butt on the concrete floor.

Slamming the cell door, the other cop looked at me and said, "Be gentle with him, Rossiter." Then they laughed like hell and left.

I went over and helped Martin to his feet. They'd worked him over pretty good. His tuxedo was all dusty and dirty, and his bow tie was twisted at a crazy angle above his rumpled, white shirt. He had a split lip, the biggest shiner since Louis K.O.'d Schmelling in their second bout, and more than a few welts and contusions marching down the length of his equine face. I also noted that he had a couple spots that looked like dried blood smeared on his cummerbund. I hadn't noticed those before.

"What happened to you?" I asked, after I'd stood him up.

"What do you think?" he said, dabbing at his swollen lips. "They gave me the third degree."

"No, I mean at the club. I couldn't find you backstage."

He shuffled over to the bunk and sat down. "I went back to find Donny. The next thing I knew, hordes of police burst in and dragged me down here." He paused, grimacing a bit as he felt at the largest welt over his left eye. Then he continued, his voice rising with each word he spoke. "They wouldn't believe me when I said I didn't know where Donny was. Wouldn't believe me when I told them I didn't kill Trixie. Damn them anyway! They wouldn't even let me call my attorney."

"Donny flew the coop, huh? And you don't know where he went?"

"No."

"You sure?"

"What did I just tell you?" He gave me a foul look. "You're as bad as the cops, Rossiter, you know that?"

"I can be worse," I told him. "You better be sure you're shooting me the straight skinny."

Martin ignored my implicit threat, saying, "How can you treat me like this? I didn't have anything to do with Trixie's murder."

I studied him for a moment. "That blood on your cummerbund," I said. "Where did it come from?"

He glanced down at the brownish-red stains, his eyes growing as wide as a couple dinner plates. "Oh my God! It's Trixie's blood!" He tore the cummerbund off and threw it to the floor.

"How'd it get there?"

He took a couple deep breaths. "I tried to help Trixie. I guess I bent over her and the blood got on me."

"You guess?"

"Well, it was all crazy," he said, starting to pace back and forth in the cell. "Trixie was supposed to be onstage. I went back to find out what was keeping her. I found her lying in her dressing room. It was horrible. She had blood all over her gown."

"O.K. What about Donny? Where was he during all this?"

"He ran in and found me with Trixie. I wanted to call the cops, but Donny said I should call you instead."

"You have any clue who stuck Trixie? Any at all?"

"No."

I pulled out a Philip Morris and tamped it against my Zippo. "You own a knife, Martin?"

"No."

"Donny own one?"

25

Martin got his back up. "No, he doesn't! I don't like your insinuations. He's a sweet, loving man."

"Then why'd he rabbit?" I asked. "He ever share any of his sweet love with Trixie, perchance?"

Martin screamed something unintelligible and suddenly rushed me, throwing a wild windmill of punches. Startled, I picked most of them off, but got clipped in the chin by a surprisingly decent right. I wrapped him up in a bear hug and held on until the fight went out of him.

"I'm going to let go of you, now. If you swing on me again, I'll swing back."

"I'm sorry, I'm sorry," he said, as I let loose of him. He staggered across the cell and threw himself on his bunk and began to cry. "Donny's *true blue*. He's never cheated on me. We never even have a cross word."

"Look, pal," I said, crossing over to him. "I wasn't trying to ride you. These are just questions that need to be asked. Understand?"

He sat up and nodded, then pulled out his tuxedo's dress handkerchief and blew his nose loud and long.

The bars on the cell door suddenly clattered and clanked behind me. It was Mahoney, night guard at the jail, raking his nightstick across them as hard as he could.

"What's all the ruckus back here?" he yelled. "You two have a little lover's spat or what, Rossiter?"

"Up yours, Mahoney," I told him.

"You'd like that, wouldn't you?" he said with a sneer.

"You're a real wit."

"Just keep it down." He waved his nightstick at me. "I have to come back here, again, you won't like it."

"I don't like it, now."

Mahoney glared at me. Then he laughed and said, "Well,

26

I'll let you two get back to whatever you were doing. Just remember what I told you." He took off up the hall.

"Where the hell's my lawyer?" I hollered after him.

Martin came over and stood next to me by the cell door. "I want to call my lawyer, too! I have the right to a phone call!"

Too late. Mahoney was long gone. Martin grasped the metal bars with both hands and shook the hell out of the door. "I don't like this! I don't like being locked up!"

"Don't go wigging out on me again," I told him. "Things are bad enough. We're here until morning from the looks of it. Miss Jenkins will have my lawyer on the ball, though. I'll have him get you out, too. Don't worry."

"I know, I know . . . ." He stalked back to his bunk. "I'm just beside myself about Donny, that's all. Where could he be? You've got to find him when you get out of here."

"Believe me," I said, "it's already high on my agenda." I offered him one of my smokes. He declined. "Let's talk more about Trixie. How long had he worked for you?"

"Well, we've known her for a few years. But, officially, she'd just started on the payroll. She won our last amateur drag contest, and we'd just signed her to a six-month contract."

"Never had any trouble with him?"

"None whatsoever."

"Any enemies that you know of?"

"Enemies? Trixie? Of course not."

"Did he owe money to anybody? Gamble? Play the ponies heavy like you and Donny, maybe?"

"No, no, and no," Martin said emphatically. "Trixie was perfect. Beautiful. She didn't have any vices at all."

"Nobody's perfect, my friend," I said. "Everybody's got vices, and everybody's got some kind of troubles."

27

"What's that supposed to mean?"

"Just what I said. If you want me to get a line on who killed Trixie, you need to be more realistic. Way you make it sound, he was prettier than Betty Grable, sweeter than molasses, and holier than the Pope. They just don't make 'em that way."

"But it's the truth. I swear it."

"What did Trixie do for a living?"

"Oh, she was pretty poor. Never had hardly any money—only worked part time as a cabana boy at the Camlin Hotel."

I stubbed out my butt on the concrete floor. "You sure you're not holding anything back on me, Martin?"

"Of course not."

"If you are, I'll find it."

He went silent.

"So, Donny left you holding the bag. Just skipped out on you."

Finally, he spoke up in a subdued voice. "It's happened before," he said. "Him skipping out. Donny's a busy man, but sometimes he just disappears. Says he's going out for a pack of smokes and doesn't come back for an hour."

"That so?"

He paused, a worried look coming over his face. "Unfortunately," he said. "Sometimes, when the phone rings and I get it, there's just silence on the other end of the line."

"Really?"

"Yes. It's been going on for over a year."

"Seems a tad suspicious," I said. "Don't you think?"

He didn't respond.

"C'mon, Martin. Doesn't sound so true blue to me. Spill it. What's the real story with you and Donny?"

"Oh, all right," he said, gritting his teeth like it was a real effort to give me a straight answer. "I lied. The truth is I'm afraid Donny's been cheating on me."

"Tell me more," I said, offering him a smoke again, which he accepted this time around.

I was just getting it lit for him, when a big, low voice boomed out from the cell door. "Rossiter! What the devil are you doing here?"

It was Haggerty, my attorney, two hundred and fifty plus pounds of legal legerdemain. I jumped to my feet.

"Didn't Miss Jenkins call you?" I asked him.

"No."

"Then what are *you* doing here?"

He gave me an odd look, kind of edgy-like, and glanced past me toward Martin.

"I'm sure glad to see you," said Martin, coming up beside me.

"What?" I asked him. "You know Haggerty, too?"

"I certainly should," Martin told me. "He's my attorney."

"Your attorney? He's my attorney."

"I represent both of you," said Haggerty.

"Well, that's a coincidence," I said. "So, what the hell? Spring us both, already."

"Well, um . . . " Haggerty mumbled. "I'm afraid there's a bit of a problem there Jake, old top."

"Oh, yeah?" I asked, wondering about this uncharacter-istic wishy-washiness from my normally ultra-confident and gregarious mouthpiece. "Like what?"

"Cops think you were involved in this murder, Jake. Even so, if I'd known you were in here, I could have gotten you sprung. As it is, I've only got bail arranged for Martin. You're going to have to wait until the morning."

"Bullshit," I told him. "Bullshit!"

I repeated the word, and several other choice ones, while the jailer showed up with the keys and let Martin out. He and Haggerty skipped up the hall to freedom, leaving me alone in the cell, except for my thoughts about the situation—all of them foul, and some downright depressing.

It felt like the cards were all stacked against me. Everything on this case was going to shit right from the get-go. I'd barely begun looking into it, and here I was, detoured to the slammer and accused of murder.

If I didn't know better, this could be the set-up for one of those cynical, grade-B, crime flicks that Miss Jenkins was always dragging me out to see. Every character in them made one dumb decision after another, and always ended up going down the tubes.

Well, I'd been a private dick too long to buy into that crap. What you did in this life counted for something.

All I had to do was get back on track. I didn't roll over for anybody or anything. I just had to get out ahead of the game. Make things play *my* way.

Chapter

3

I CAME OUT OF A RESTLESS SLEEP THE NEXT morning, tossing, turning, and pissed. The bad dream I'd been having kept repeating in my head: I was trapped, nowhere to run, nowhere to hide, everything closing in on me. Worse, I couldn't do a single thing about it, just lie there and take it. Man, I hadn't felt that way since I was stuck in a foxhole on Guadalcanal facing my first Banzai charge.

Added to those rotten feelings, some monkey was playing my jail cell bars like a xylophone.

"Mahoney, cut it—" I started to say, then saw that it was Miss Jenkins, noisily raking her silver makeup compact back and forth across the bars.

"I always wanted to do that," she said with a crafty smile, as I jumped out of my bunk. "Ever since I saw that movie, *The Big House.*"

"Yeah, well, the cons did that with their tin cups, not their damned compacts," I told her, straightening out my rumpled suit coat as best I could. "Where the hell's Haggerty?"

Lt. Baker walked up beside Miss Jenkins. "Morning, Jake." He tipped his hat to me. "You look like hell."

"Get me out of here."

"That's just what we're doing." He held up a big, brass key

ring, selected one of the keys and unlocked my cell. "There. You're officially sprung."

"We posted bail," said Miss Jenkins. "Lt. Baker saw the judge first thing and vouched for you."

"And we were lucky to get it, considering the circumstances," Baker told me. "I'm up for captain in a couple months, Jake. Don't do anything to screw me up."

"Who, me?" I grabbed my hat and beat feet out of the cell, saying, "I'd like to take my private dick license and shove it down the throats of the moron cops who hauled me in."

"Don't blame them, they were just doing their job," said Baker as I put on my fedora and got it adjusted. "Oh, before I forget... Happy birthday."

"Yes, happy birthday," echoed Miss Jenkins.

"Only thing happy about it," I said, "will be getting out of this place."

"Look," she told me, putting the compact back into her purse and withdrawing a white, business-sized envelope with my name on it.

"What's that? A present?"

"Sort of." She handed me the envelope. "A man brought it by the office just after I got in this morning."

"A man? What man?"

"Open it up," she said. "It'll improve your mood."

I did as directed. Found five, crisp C-notes inside. I like lots of moola with my name on it, but I still repeated my former question. "O.K., who brought it? Did he give a name?"

"Bennington," said Miss Jenkins. "Royce Bennington."

"I don't know any Benningtons," I said. "Let alone one named Royce. Why would he give me this dough?"

"Donny."

"Donny?"

"Bennington advanced the money on behalf of Donny," Miss Jenkins told me. "Enough to cover our fees for a week at double our normal rate. Plus the extra that took care of your bail."

"Seems a little hinky," I said, but slipped the dough into my breast pocket anyway. "I need a shower and a shave."

I headed up the hall, eager to leave my night in the slammer as far behind as possible. Lt. Baker caught up to me before Miss Jenkins did.

"Looks a little suspicious, Jake, getting all that dough from a wanted man," he said, unlocking the main cellblock door for me.

"That a statement, or some kind of accusation?" I asked.

"Take it any way you want. Look, Jake, I've got my butt on the line for you."

"You know I had nothing to do with this."

"Doesn't matter. You've made plenty of enemies on the force over the years. This is just the kind of excuse they need to try and stick it to you."

He got the door open, and I blew through it without a reply.

I beat it out onto the street where I took a deep breath of the slightly salt-tinged air from nearby Elliott Bay and thought it had never smelled so damned good.

"My car's right down the hill on First Avenue," said Miss Jenkins, cinching up her floral print scarf against the morning breeze.

"I'll walk along with you," Baker said, a freshly lit Old Gold between his lips. Starting down the steep half block to First, he added, "I've got some men over checking out this Bennington's place, as we speak. I doubt they'll find Donny sitting at his breakfast table, but it's worth a look-see. What's going on, anyway? How's Bennington involved in this?"

"If I knew, I'd tell you," I said.

"Fair enough," Baker told me, even though he looked like he didn't believe me. "But Bennington's name came up more than once back when I was on vice."

"How so?"

"Nothing in particular. It just came up. But my radar always starts working when a name repeats itself like that. I'm just saying watch your step, that's all."

We reached the bottom of the hill, where I spotted Miss Jenkins's coupe parked half a block up the street.

"C'mon, Jake," said Baker. "You must know something."

"Why the pressure? If I didn't know better, I'd say you didn't trust me."

"I've got pressure, too," said Baker. "Major dragnet out on my watch. Damned sordid business. Brass wants it handled fast and quiet. I need every tidbit I can get."

"O.K. Here's what I've got: Martin says he's innocent. Says Donny's innocent, too."

"That's not much."

"That's what I told you," I said.

As we reached the car, Miss Jenkins asked, "Lt. Baker?"

"Yeah?"

"Being Jake's birthday and all, do you think you could give him a little present?"

"Like what?"

She smiled her coy smile, which usually meant her wheels were turning overtime. "Oh, just this Royce Bennington's address. I couldn't find it anywhere."

Baker returned her smile, his own grin a bit coy. "You think he'll share any info he might dig up?"

"If he won't, I will," she said.

"Good enough for me." Baker pulled out his pocket note-book, copied the address onto one of its small pages, then ripped it out and gave it to her.

"Thanks," I said, snatching it out of her hand.

Miss Jenkins unlocked the passenger side, and I climbed in. As she went around and got into the driver's seat, I unrolled my window and asked Baker, "This squeeze from the brass that you mentioned: you think it's from the homo-sexual nature of this case, or from the kind of graft that keeps clubs like the Garden of Allah open?"

"Both," he said, with a grim look on his face.

"Thought so."

"Just don't leave town. O.K., Jake?"

I turned to Miss Jenkins. "Home, Jeeves."

We'd driven a couple blocks at her customary breakneck pace, when I said, "Pretty slick getting that address out of Baker, doll."

"Thanks," she said, with a quick toss of her head. "Say!" she exclaimed, causing the Plymouth to momentarily swerve dangerously close to the centerline. "I think I just realized who this Royce Bennington is."

"Clue me," I said, after she got the car under control again.

She gave me a sly glance. "Think mink. Think ermine and sable, too."

I thought, but it didn't take long. "Bennington Furs!"

"Voila!"

"Of course. Oldest and biggest furrier west of the Missis-sippi. We should've thought of that sooner."

"He must be worth a fortune."

"Several fortunes," I said. "Like Donny."

Coming to a hard stop at a red light, Miss Jenkins said, "I wonder what else they have in common."

"Maybe Donny and Martin like furs."

"You think so?"

"We'll do our best to find out. Right after I have my shower and shave."

Freshly cleaned and coifed, the Lilac Vegetal splashed liberally on my kisser ridding the last of the jail stink from me, I stepped out of my bedroom to find Miss Jenkins just hanging up the phone at my desk. I smiled as I knotted up my best blue tie.

"You've been busy, I see."

"Indeed," she said.

I sauntered over to the desk. "Let me guess—you've already got a line on Donny, and fingered the prime suspect in Trixie's murder."

"Better," she said, giving me a wide smile. "I managed to get us new reservations for your birthday dinner. On short notice, too."

"Doll," I said. "I'm supposed to be going out with Heine tonight. He was tied up, couldn't celebrate my real birthday yesterday."

"*Neither could I!*" she snapped, taking me aback.

"Well, I was in jail, I couldn't—"

"I still want to take you out whether it's your real birthday today or not," she said, looking hurt. "Doesn't that mean anything? I've planned this dinner for—"

"O.K.," I said. "Fine. I'll cancel. He'll understand."

She looked much improved.

"Where the hell *is* Heine, anyway?" I asked. "Have you

heard from him? He should have finished up the Horowitz case by now. How long can it take to get photos of a cheating wife?"

"Haven't heard a word," Miss Jenkins said, standing up from my desk, but not before absently straightening out most of the paper piles on it, which I hated her doing because I never could find anything afterwards. "No phone calls and nothing from the answering service either."

"That's not like him," I said, wondering why my best pal in the whole world seemed to be standing me up. "Put in a call to the answering service and leave Heine a message. Tell him to get hold of us and let us know what's up. O.K.?"

"Right away," she said. But instead of picking up the phone, she came around the desk and started fiddling with my tie. "Your knot's all wrong," Miss Jenkins told me, smelling of the ritzy Chanel perfume I'd given her last Christmas. "It's not tight enough, and you've got it off-center."

"Quit fussing with me," I said, though I sometimes liked her fussing with me.

"Hold still," she said. I obeyed the command. "Got it. Now, that wasn't so bad, was it?"

"I've had worse."

She locked eyes with me for a second, then gave me a playful sock in the gut. "See if I come to your rescue again if your tie's crooked."

"Bet you will."

She grinned, then headed for the outer office. "I'll go put in that call for Heine."

"You do that."

Pausing at the door, she turned back to me. "Oh, by the way ..."

"What is it?"

"You missed a button, too," she said, pointing at my mid-section. "Fourth one down."

I checked under my tie. She was right. Buttoning my shirt, I said, "What would I do without you?"

"That's exactly right." Then she chuckled and left.

Miss Jenkins. What a pip. She was pursuing my birthday dinner with the same tenacity she exhibited on our cases. She'd turned into quite a bulldog ever since she'd gotten her private detective license a couple years back. A little temper-amental at times, but a very attractive and beguiling bulldog, even so.

I buzzed her on the intercom.

"We have to stop meeting like this," came her reply, followed by a slight snicker.

"What are you up to for the rest of the day?" I asked.

"Mostly paperwork. Louie might have some more work for us. I have to check back with him at some point."

"Good. I need you to do something for me. I want you to put in a call to O'Brien, the police photographer, and see if you can get him to—"

"Already done," she said.

"What?"

"I called him this morning. I knew you'd want a photo of the crime scene."

"Oh…" I said, marveling at her mind-reading abilities. "Good thinking."

"I thought so."

"So, what's the upshot?"

"O'Brien's printing copies. He hemmed and hawed at first, but jumped right to it when Lt. Baker got on the line with me. I'm supposed to pick them up in about an hour."

"O.K.," I told her. "I've got another place for you to go as soon as you get them."

"Where?"

"Straight over to the Garden of Allah. Find the spot where Trixie was killed and compare the photos to it. Scour it good for any clues the cops might have missed."

"Good idea," she said. "But aren't you coming? What if nobody's there? How am I supposed to get in?"

"Use that set of skeleton keys I gave you. That's what they're for."

"Oh, of course. I forgot about them. But where are you going to be?"

"I'll be downtown visiting the morgue," I told her, finishing off the last of my Cutty Sark-laced coffee. "Doc Prescott owes me one. I want a closer look at Trixie's body," I added. "But first, I'm going to pay a call on this Royce Bennington. I don't know if I trust him."

Chapter

4

I ROLLED UP OUTSIDE ROYCE BENNINGTON'S digs on the west slope of Capitol Hill. To call the place a mansion would've been an understatement. Describing it as a palace would be more on the money. Constructed of a light, rose-colored marble, with a dark red tile roof, it was two stories high, and about the size of an Essex-class aircraft carrier.

I wheeled the Roadmaster up the long, main drive, past the many graceful elms and maples that lined the way. Scads of beautiful, white marble, Greek-style nude statues dotted the grounds. Everything about the place dripped class. Same for the big, brand new Packard limo sitting off to the side, under a large weeping willow tree. A liveried chauffeur was waxing the ritzy ride. He tipped his hat as I drove past, then went back to rubbing the lustrous, black beast.

A bright red Jaguar sports car was parked by the main entrance to the house. I pulled in behind it, got out and went up the steps. They were flanked by two alabaster cherubs, both peeing into the small fountains set on either side of the front door.

I'd barely rung the bell, when the door swung open, and an elderly, black-suited butler asked, "May I help you, sir?"

"I'm here to see Royce Bennington."

"Have you an appointment?"

I handed him one of my business cards. "Give him this. Tell him it's about Donny. He'll see me."

"Very well." He motioned me inside.

The large foyer was painted a rich cream color. I followed the butler's lead across the mosaic floor, which depicted some sort of Roman Bacchanalia: semi-nude men and women and satyrs all cavorting and sucking down the fruit of the vine like there was no tomorrow.

"This way, sir," he said.

We headed down a dim hallway, lined with stuffed and mounted heads of various types of big game: lions, tigers, leopards, water buffalo, gazelle, a rhino, and even an enormous African elephant head over the door to the study. The taxidermist had done a bang-up job: they were utterly life-like, especially their eyes, which seemed to track you as you went past them. It was a little eerie, actually, in the low light—the many predators all snarling, their lips curled back and their big fangs bared, ready for action.

The butler left me in the study with the words: "Make yourself comfortable, Mr. Rossiter."

I moseyed around looking at the various exhibits. There were more stuffed animal heads, but the study was really like a museum of weapons. One wall was covered with glass-fronted gun cabinets containing nearly every type of rifle under the sun—hunting rifles of various calibers, including a couple big-bore elephant guns, pump and double barreled shotguns, several lever-action Winchesters, plus a large .453 bolt-action, and one custom-made Italian target rifle. Off in the far corner, stood a gun cabinet devoted entirely to collectibles. Among others, it held a number of flintlock muskets, a vintage Spencer buffalo gun, an old 30/40 Krag, a couple early Springfields, and a pristine Model 1896 German Mauser, essentially the same bolt-action rifle that the krauts had used in both WW I and WWII.

I didn't know anything about Bennington, except what Baker had told me, but I *did* like his gun collection. If guns were the only measure of the man, he might turn out O.K.

A pair of crossed, Arabian-style swords, their gold handles encrusted with precious stones, hung over the fireplace. The other wall displayed a knife and sword collection. There were Calvary sabers, broadswords, rapiers, cutlasses, daggers, dirks, switchblades, and stilettos.

I noticed that a knife seemed to be missing from the collection. Its mounting bracket was empty, and the wall was a slightly lighter shade where it had been, leaving a faint outline of the type of blade that had been there: a large, curved blade with a wide grip.

All of a sudden, the knives on the wall shook slightly. Were we having an earthquake, I wondered? Then one of the bookshelf panels swung open, and out popped this gorgeous dame, early-twenties at most, with long, wavy chestnut hair, and totally naked under her transparent negligee.

"Oh, hello," she said, nonchalantly. "I'm sorry if I startled you."

"I'm not." I gave her curvaceous figure a healthy gander.

"What's your name?" she asked.

"Jake. Jake Rossiter. What's yours?"

Her eyes twinkled. "Wouldn't you like to know?" Then she giggled and disappeared back through the panel as quick as she'd come.

"Hold on—" I started to say, but the panel swung shut

before I could get out another word. I pushed and prodded on the panel, but try as I might, I couldn't get the thing to open up again.

I was still fiddling with it, when a voice behind me said, "You must be Mr. Rossiter."

I spun around. "Yeah, that's me."

"Higgins gave me your card. I'm Royce Bennington." The man smiled and approached me. "Sorry to keep you waiting."

He was about forty or so, movie-star handsome, with every hair in his black pompadour perfectly in place. He wore a deep blue smoking jacket, red ascot, and a pair of soft leather slippers. He extended his manicured hand, and I shook it. He had a firm grip. So much so, that the big, gold signet ring he wore bit into my knuckles and caused me to take back my hand earlier than usual.

"I hope you've been comfortable," he said.

"Sure," I told him. "I've had some entertainment, too. Young woman wearing virtually nothing greeted me just before you did. Dames make a habit of popping out of your walls around here?"

He laughed. "Ah, I see you've met our resident nymph."

"Nymph?"

"Yes. She flits here, flits there, flits everywhere." He stepped up to the panel and pressed a spot near its bottom. As it swung open, he gestured for me to take a look inside. Wasn't much to see. Just a dark passageway that ran in about six feet, then took a sharp right. "My father built this house at the turn of the century," he continued. "He put in all the secret doors and passageways. Our nymph seems to love them." He winked at me. "She just wasn't ready to go home after the party last night, that's all."

"O.K.," I said, as if his explanation actually explained much. "I see you've got quite a knife collection."

"Yes. I've collected various types of weapons for years. Little hobby of mine."

"I couldn't help but notice that one's missing," I said, pointing to the empty spot in the collection.

He frowned. "That disappeared a couple weeks ago."

"Stolen?"

"Perhaps. I've had my butler search high and low, but it hasn't shown up."

"Hope it wasn't too valuable."

"It was, actually. A 12th century Saracen dagger. The finest Damascus steel. Pristine condition."

"That's too bad." I studied him. "I hope it shows up again."

Bennington's smile returned. "So, to what pleasure do I owe your company, Mr. Rossiter? Donny, I assume?"

"Yeah," I said. "Is he one of your guests, too?"

"No, I'm afraid not," he said. "So, you're a friend of Donny's?"

"That's right. What's with this money you gave to my partner?"

"The five hundred dollars?"

"Yeah."

"I advanced it on behalf of Donny. Didn't she tell you that?"

"Yeah, but—"

"What, Mr. Rossiter?" He smiled. "Are you saying now that you've had some of its benefits you don't want it?"

"Not exactly."

"Care for a smoke?"

"Don't mind if I do." I reached for my Philip Morrises.

"No, no," he said. "I mean a real smoke. Come with me."

He turned and beckoned me to the door. "We can continue our discussion in comfort."

I followed him out into the hall, thinking he was leading me off to some fancy smoking room and a good cigar. Cigars I could take or leave, expensive or not, but I liked the brandy that usually came with them.

He led me past several closed doors, up a wide staircase, and down a long hall to a ten-foot tall, intricately carved teak door.

Opening it up, Bennington said, "After you, Mr. Rossiter."

I went in and found myself in a scene that could have been taken right out of the Arabian Nights: a circular room, only about fifteen feet in diameter, with a big water pipe in the middle of it, surrounded by tons of large, multi-colored, fringed pillows. The room was totally covered with Persian carpets, rich silks, and many fine tapestries, including one that billowed down from where it had been draped across the ceiling. It showed the most beautiful garden imaginable, overflowing with lush greenery, bubbling fountains, flying doves, glittering jewels, and golden minarets that soared straight up into the bluest sky I'd ever seen.

"I see you like that," said Bennington, as I gawked at the tapestry. "It's a depiction of the Muslim Paradise. The finest I've ever come across. It's called the *Garden of Allah*."

I thought about the irony of the name, then said, "Well, if that's what Heaven looks like, I might have to change my ways."

"Indeed," he replied. "Well, sit Mr. Rossiter. Be comfortable. I have the hookah filled and ready. I guarantee you the most pleasurable smoke of your life."

I settled down onto one of the big pillows, and stared at the tall water pipe and the numerous smoking tubes that

extended out from every side of it like so many dark, slith-
ering snakes. "I've only seen these things in pictures," I said.
"Never smoked one."

"Then it will be a real treat." He settled down on a group
of pillows across from me. "I use only the finest, strong
Turkish blend. But the water cools it to the smoothest
perfection. Before we start, though, let me ring for some
coffee." He reached up and pulled twice on the long, tasseled,
velvet cord that hung down beside him. "Turkish, too, of
course. The experience wouldn't be the same without it."

"Of course," I agreed, thinking that the water pipe might
be better than a cigar, but I'd still prefer the brandy to coffee.
Turkish or otherwise.

Bennington took a smoking tube in his mouth, lit one of
the long stick matches that lay next to the water pipe, and
started to fire the thing up. The water bubbling in the clear
glass urn, pungent smoke curling from his lips, he paused,
took the silver-tipped tube from his mouth, and said, "Now,
for your questions about Donny, Mr. Rossiter. I shall be
happy to oblige. Try the hookah, though." He reached across
and passed one of the smoking tubes to me. "Here. It's easy.
Just take it in your mouth and suck."

I locked eyes with him for a moment and tried to read his
expression, but couldn't see anything but a general friendli-
ness. "I think I'll just puff on it," I told him.

He threw me a wry smile. I took a tentative drag. The
smoke was good. Damned good. Very rich, very strong, yet
cool and mellow as advertised.

"So," I said. "What's your association with Donny?"

"I've known him for years," he said, reclining a bit into
the pillows. "My parents knew his parents, as well. We're old
friends."

I puffed on the water pipe a moment. "You mentioned a party. You throw a lot of parties, Mr. Bennington?"

"Oh, all the time. 'Eat, drink, and be merry...' You know how that saying goes. As a matter of fact, I'm having another get together soon. Perhaps you'd care to attend."

"Maybe," I said, starting to feel oddly mellow. Maybe there *was* something to what he said about a water pipe being relaxing, after all. "Well, I guess I should thank you for passing that bail money along for me."

"Don't mention it.." He took a particularly long drag on the pipe. "Say, I'm curious," he said.

"About what?"

"Your profession. What's your weapon of choice, Mr. Rossiter?"

"No weapon at all," I said. "If I'm lucky."

His eyes narrowed. "What if you're not lucky?"

".45 Colt semi-auto. Haven't met anyone it can't stop."

"Do you like hunting?"

"Get enough of it in my line of work."

He laughed. Laughed a little too hard and a little too long, I thought. "That's unfortunate. I'm a big game hunter, myself."

"I noticed," I said, thinking about his menagerie of stuffed heads.

"If you ever change your mind, you're most welcome on my next safari."

"I'll keep it in mind," I told him.

As I puffed away on the hookah, I felt very relaxed and comfortable. This Bennington seemed a decent sort after all—polite, personable, gracious. Whatever Baker said about him, this guy knew and talked guns: my kind of talk.

I opened my mouth to ask him something else, but somehow lost the thought. I strained for it, but for the life of me couldn't catch it. That was unusual—I was always on track in my questioning.

"Do you like the hookah, Mr. Rossiter?" Bennington asked.

"Yeah … It's smooth," I said, feeling a little light-headed. "Maybe too smooth … "

He smiled. "That would be the hashish."

"*The what?*"

"Hashish," he said, calmly. "It's part of my Turkish blend."

I sat up straight. "What the hell? That's illegal you know."

"Not unless somebody tells." He sat up straight, too. Leaned in toward me. "You're not going to tell, are you?"

I stood up, my legs feeling unsteady—thought about slugging him, but didn't quite feel up to it. "This is some kind of crap," I said. "I'm going. You and I will talk some other time."

He stood. "I'm sorry you feel that way," he told me. "I thought we might be kindred spirits."

"Not on your life, pal."

"Let me see you out, Mr. Rossiter."

"I'll find the door myself," I told him.

"Do come back again," he said warmly, as I left the room.

I'm not sure how long it took me to find my way out of that huge, labyrinthine house. Seemed like hours. But I finally found an exit. I got into the Roadmaster and drove off. The car seemed to be standing still, but the landscape was floating by the windows like a movie screen. For some reason, I found that funny. Laughed my butt off about it. Laughed all the way to the City Morgue.

Chapter

5

I ROLLED UP TO THE CITY MORGUE STILL feeling part way out on queer street. It wasn't like I'd never tried any reefer—a few jazzmen I knew in my bootlegging days had enticed me to have a few puffs of the weed—but what Royce Bennington had slipped me in the hookah was different, way more powerful. Hashish. Sure, I'd heard of it. But now that I'd had some, I knew to stay forever clear of the stuff: it made you feel so damned good that you just naturally wanted more.

I took a few healthy slugs of Scotch from my hip flask to try and counter the lingering affects of the happy crap, then moseyed on in to visit my friend the coroner.

"Rossiter," said Doctor Phillip Prescott, standing next to a sparkling clean, stainless steel examining table, and puffing his ever-present briar. "You can't just barge in here while I'm doing an autopsy. How many times have I told you?"

"Looks like you're through with whatever stiff you were slicing," I told him. "Don't think I've ever seen that table looking so clean."

"Be that as it may," he said. "I have the next coming right up—yet another in the great pantheon of corpses that roll through this under-funded establishment."

"Life's tough."

The barest trace of a smile crossed his crotchety features. "So, Rossiter, where you go, trouble usually follows. What variety have you brought me today?"

"Female impersonator named Trixie," I said as we shook hands. "Didn't get his real name. Multiple stab wounds. Body should have come in yesterday. Ring any bells?"

"An entire church full. I tend not to forget men who have their faces painted up like French whores. Lawrence Leland Murphy; that's his Christian name. Quite attractive, though, in his own way. What's your interest?" He smiled broadly. "Professional, I hope."

I ignored his jibe. "Case I'm working." I lit up a smoke to try to mask the strong disinfectant smell that permeated the morgue. "Like to get a look at him, if I could. Maybe get an earful of your autopsy results, too. You cut him open yet?"

"Sewed him up right after my one and only coffee break this morning." Doc Prescott took the pipe out of his mouth, then let out a big sigh. He suddenly looked two decades older than his sixty-odd years. Slowly shaking his head, he said, "I'm tired, Rossiter. Just plain pooped. My morning java doesn't seem to perk me up anymore."

"Maybe you need a vacation."

"Too many dead people. The town's just full of them."

"How about a pick-me-up, doc?" I pulled out my hip flask and offered it to him.

"I'm off the sauce," he said, waving the flask away, but keeping his eyes fixed on it like a bird dog ready to flush a pheasant. "It's been well over a year, now. I can assure you that I still greatly miss it."

"Oh, I forgot," I said. Prescott had nearly lost his job because of lushing it up. I put the flask away after taking a sip. "These things can take awhile."

"So they say." He straightened up and threw me a little grin. "Perhaps you should think about drying out, too. See for yourself how horrible it is to live without it."

"Nah."

He gave me a look.

"How about the stiff?" I asked. "I'd like to get a look at him before the cocktail hour."

"We wouldn't want to miss that, now would we?" He smoothed out the lapels on his white laboratory jacket, then gestured for me to follow him. "Come this way. You can pull the late Mr. Murphy out of the fridge while I go and get my autopsy notes."

I followed him back to the rear of the big examining room, where a bank of coolers was built into the far wall. There, he pointed out cooler #3 and told me to have at it.

By the time Doc Prescott returned from his office, I had the steel cart bearing Trixie's remains hauled out into the middle of the green tile floor. He was slit open from just above his privates to his breastbone, then stitched up again like a freshly stuffed turkey about to go into the oven.

"We save the delicate stitch-work for the living," said Prescott.

"I see you left Trixie's makeup on."

"Yes." He spent a moment appraising Trixie's heavy pan-cake makeup and even heavier mascara and dark penciled eyebrows and flaming red, extra-glossy lipstick. "I thought it quite a nice touch. The pallor of death is so ubiquitous around this place, it's rather pleasing to see a pretty face."

Doc was right, though I'd have never admitted it. Tall and lithe, Trixie had very fine, almost feminine features: a narrow, well-shaped nose, high and refined cheekbones, and a thin waist, with extremely long, nicely proportioned, shaven legs. If I managed to ignore the equipment between said legs, he was a very attractive woman.

"He was wearing a lovely red gown when they brought him in," said Prescott. "What a shame it was ruined from all the stab wounds; it must have been extremely expensive."

Speaking of stab wounds, I appraised them next. Counted over a dozen of them on Trixie's body: chest, stomach, and a few in his left side. They were ugly. Very ugly—dark maroon punctures, varying in width from about an inch to two inches, each surrounded by vivid purple blotches that radiated out around the wounds. Reminded me of the bayonet wounds some of our boys took in the Pacific, including myself once on Iwo—took it in the upper thigh; hurt like gangbusters; but not as much as my own bayonet hurt the lousy Jap who'd stuck it to me.

"Poor fellow was stabbed fourteen times," offered Prescott, referring to his notes. He went around the table opposite me, then flipped to another page in his clipboard. "Any one of the six deepest penetrations could have proved fatal."

"Know which one did?" I asked.

"Yes, actually. It was the wound just to the left of his sternum. The blade completely severed his aorta. Death would have been almost instantaneous."

"I see. Fair bet, then, that it would have been the last wound he took, huh?"

"No, oddly enough," Prescott said. "It's hard to gauge, but from the general lividity and such, my educated guess is that the stab wound by his sternum was the *first* wound he suffered. The rest were post mortem."

"So, whoever went after him just kept stabbing him after he was dead."

"Correct."

"What are the odds you're wrong about that, doc?"

He tamped the tobacco down in his pipe a little better. "Oh, about the same as a three-legged horse winning the daily double at Longacres."

I laughed. "Wish I had the same precision in my line of work."

"The dead don't lie," he said. "I often think it would be more interesting if they did."

There was something odd about Trixie's hands and forearms. They didn't seem to have so much as a single nick or scratch on them. I hadn't noticed that when I first saw his body backstage at the club. Then again, I didn't get much of a look at him fast as the flatfeet had grabbed me up.

"He hasn't got any defensive wounds, doc," I said, lifting each of his hands and carefully examining the palms and underside of his arms.

"No, he doesn't," said Prescott. "I noticed that myself."

"He must have really been surprised by someone," I mused. "Either that or maybe he knew and trusted the person who rubbed him out."

"There is a third possibility, Rossiter."

"Yeah? What's that?"

"That he was surprised when the person he knew and trusted stabbed him."

I was a little slow on the uptake, but I finally got it. "Say, that's not bad, doc. First joke I've heard you crack in a long time."

Most people laugh at their own jokes. Even when they aren't funny. Not Doc Prescott. "Well," he said. "Don't wait around for the next one."

"You got Trixie's home address handy?" I asked.

"It's here in the paperwork," he said, going to the first page on his clipboard. "I don't suppose it would hurt to give it to you."

"Won't hurt me," I told him. "Certainly won't hurt Trixie."

He didn't comment on my poor attempt at levity. Just rattled off the address, which I wrote into my pocket notebook.

"Just one more question? These stab wounds... Could they have been caused by a curved blade about eight inches long and a couple inches wide at the base?"

"Indeed," he said, without even referring to his notes. "Your description fits the parameters of the wounds quite nicely. Especially the curvature of the blade. The interior damage could have only been caused by such a curved instrument. Have you the suspect blade for comparison?"

"No, I don't. The one I'm thinking of is missing."

"Good. That's one less thing for me to do today." He flipped his clipboard closed. My signal to leave.

"Well, thanks, doc. I'll be motoring. If I have any other questions, I'll—"

"*Call first*," he said, firmly. "And do try not to send me any extra bodies this week, will you?"

"I'll do my best." I offered him my hand, but he turned and headed toward his office. "Take care of yourself," I called after him.

"Nobody else will," he mumbled over his shoulder.

With that, he disappeared into his office at the back of

the autopsy room. I followed suit the other direction. Hit the sidewalk outside the morgue, then hit my hip flask fairly hard. A visit to the morgue often had that effect on me. A visit with Doc Prescott *always* had that effect on me. He was getting to be more like a zombie every time I saw him. You hung around him and his establishment too long, that walking dead quality threatened to rub off on you.

As I took my second long pull off the flask, I knew that's what Prescott was probably doing back in his little tomb of an office. He'd had a hard time of it lately. Said he'd gotten off the sauce, but I'd smelled it on his breath right enough. For Prescott, the booze was turning into so much embalming fluid. For me, it was high-test ethyl.

Bennington's missing knife had to be the key to this case. Its similarity to the murder weapon was just too coincidental. But even though my search for the blade was just starting and a little low on gas, I didn't let it worry me much. All I had to do was top off my tank and turn over every rock along the road.

Chapter

6

I STEERED THE ROADMASTER UPTOWN AND decided not to get too far ahead of myself, however. It didn't pay in this game. You made many assumptions early on, you could start discounting possibilities and end up having them blindside you later on. All I had to do at this juncture was to cover all the bases and make the right plays as they came up.

Good old legwork was what was called for, and I had plenty of players to pinch-hit if I needed them. Miss Jenkins should've wrapped up her skip-trace for Louie the bail bonds-man and be landing a fat percentage of Thomas "Blinky" Todd's jumped bail. And Heine should be about done with his investigation of Abe Horowitz's cheating wife, Lorna. Plus, I had Manny Velcker and Vic Croce to fill out my roster if I needed them. I could bring my whole team into play at almost a moment's notice. Plus, I could afford it, for a change, with all the extra dough our cases were bringing in this month.

I checked my pocket notebook: 612 Summit Avenue, #12, was the address I'd gotten from Doc Prescott. I goosed it up Third Avenue, turned east at Denny Way, and headed for Capitol Hill.

The apartment building was located near the corner of Summit and Pike, about six blocks south of Denny. Denny was kind of a dividing line between nice and not so nice. North of Denny Way, you got decent, to nice, to even fancy apartment buildings and houses. South of Denny, the streets— Summit, Bellevue, Boylston, etc.—held places mostly like Trixie's building: dumps. They ranged from boarding houses, to run-down shacks, to old, decrepit apartment buildings, most of which featured only efficiency units, since even one-bedrooms were more than the traffic could bear for the neighborhood.

Trixie's joint appeared to be no exception—a small, two-story, wood-framed building, with shake siding, settling unevenly on its foundation, which looked like it hadn't seen a fresh coat of paint since well before the Depression.

I parked the Roadmaster behind an old jalopy with a broken tail light, and bailed out for a good snoop. Had to dodge a couple broken bottles of vino on my way up to the steps leading to the front door.

The six wooden stairs creaked and groaned as I climbed them. A hand-painted sign on the stoop read: VACANCY, which wasn't surprising, considering that the bottom glass panel in the door was busted out and covered with a stained piece of gypsum board.

Entering the barely lit hallway, I was immediately hit with the odor of rancid cooking grease, onions, and something that smelled remarkably like stale piss—human or animal, I couldn't tell, and really didn't care to find out.

I checked the bank of brass mail boxes in what passed for a foyer. According to the numbered boxes, the building had only twelve units. Trixie's being #12, I figured it must be on the second floor. I beat feet up the nearby stairwell, found #7 at the top of the stairs, and started down toward the end of the hall.

I hadn't gone two steps, when a figure emerged from the apartment at the far end of the corridor. A woman in a red dress, wearing a matching red hat. She came out so fast, I only caught a glimpse of her before she disappeared through the fire exit on the other side of the hall.

She was long gone by the time I reached the end of the hallway, where I found the door to #12, Trixie's unit, ajar.

I stole inside, closed the door behind me, and took in my surroundings at a quick glance: a fairly large efficiency unit, just a big rectangle, with kitchenette, and a rough archway in the middle that separated the dining area from the combination living/sleeping space, which had a Murphy bed that was still pulled down from the wall. The few furnishings were old and ratty. Just a sagging sofa, a threadbare armchair, and a single side table, with lamp and yellowed shade.

Aside from that, there wasn't much else to see, except that the joint had obviously been ransacked. Every drawer and cupboard in the kitchenette was pulled open. The garbage bucket under the sink was overturned, its contents, mostly empty pork & bean and sardine tins, spilled out onto the gray linoleum. Even the breadbox on the counter was up-ended, a moldy half-loaf tipped out of it on the edge of the stained, porcelain sink.

The Murphy bed's mattress was turned over and rested at an angle on the box springs. The four built-in drawers on either side of the bed were yanked out and left that way. Whoever had rifled them had tossed their contents willy-nilly all over the bare, softwood floor. It was littered with various women's undergarments—brassieres, a couple girdles, garter belts, panties, you name it.

More women's clothes spilled out into the room from

the open closet door. Stepping over the jumble of dresses, skirts, and slips, I found four ritzy evening gowns still on their hangers in the closet and a couple open hatboxes on the single shelf at the rear.

"Who are you?" asked a man's voice behind me. "What are you doing here?"

I came out of the closet, saw the joe standing in the middle of the room.

"I could ask you the same question," I said.

He was in his mid-forties, receding hairline, clean-shaven, medium but muscular build, and dressed in a cheap suit. He gave me the once over while I checked him out.

"What have you done to this place?" he asked. "It's torn apart."

"I just got here, pal. Wasn't me."

"Why should I believe *you*?"

"And why should I believe you?" I told him. "For all I know, you trashed it."

He shook his head. "I suppose you're another of Trixie's rich pals," he muttered.

"What if I was?"

He didn't respond; stuck his hands in his pants pockets and just stared at me. His expression had gone all sulky, like a little kid who wanted to do something, but couldn't.

I pulled out my fags and offered him one. He waved it off.

I lit up. "Trixie have a lot of rich friends?"

"Too many," he said.

"I take it you're not one of them."

"I'm not rich, if that's what you mean. I have to work for a living." He paused. "What business is it of yours, anyway? Who are you?"

"Jake Rossiter," I told him. "Private heat. I'm looking into Trixie's murder. And you are?"

He clammed up. Averted his gaze.

"Don't look so guilty, pal. You do something you shouldn't have?"

He locked eyes with me again. "My name's Chuck Osbourne. I've got just as much right to be here as you do. Probably more."

"That so?"

"Yes, it is."

"Tell me, Chuck: what are *you* doing here?"

"I just came by to get a few things. Personal things that Trixie never gave back."

"State this place is in, looks like you're not the only one."

"I need to sit down," said Chuck. He headed over to the small table in the kitchenette, righted one of the overturned chairs, and sat heavily on it. "This is just too much."

I joined him at the table. "How do you know Trixie?" I asked.

"Trixie worked for me at the hotel."

"Which hotel?"

"The Camlin. I'm the assistant manager there."

"He worked for you as a cabana boy, right?"

"Yes." He gave me a suspicious glance. "How'd you know that?"

"I'm a private dick, like I said," I explained. "How long did he work for you?"

Chuck bit his lip, looked strained. "Why are you asking so many questions?"

"It's my nature," I told him. "Got some reason you don't want to answer?"

"Of course not," he said, emphatically. He pulled a pack

of Camels out of his inside pocket. Lighting one up with a small, gold Ronson, he took a deep drag, and said, "What you do is confidential, right? I can trust you, correct?"

"With your kid sister's virtue, bud."

"Look," he said. "I had a professional relationship with Trixie, that's all."

"How so?"

"I was her manager. I guided her career as a female impersonator from the very beginning. Helped her polish her act. It was finally paying off, too. She won the amateur drag contest at the Garden hands down."

"Her manager, you say."

"Yes. And that's it. You can see how that could be taken wrong if word got out—me associating with that type of person. It could even jeopardize my job."

"Well, I've always been a friend to the working man," I told him. "You've got no worries on my account."

"Good."

"Unless you haven't been square with me," I added.

"Fuck this," he said, jumping to his feet. "I told you what I know. I'm a busy man—I'm leaving."

I got up, reached across the table and grabbed him by the arm. "Hold on, I—"

Yanking me forward, all off balance, he shoved me sideways to the floor, where I landed smack on my keester.

"Fuck you!" he yelled, then bolted from the room. Sprinted away so fast that by the time I got up and out to the hallway, he was gone.

I ran out the fire exit and down the stairs, but didn't spot him anywhere, inside or out. At length, I went back up to Trixie's apartment. I probably wouldn't get any more out of Chuck right now even if I had caught him. He was just too worked up. Even though I wouldn't mind giving him a quid pro quo to his own keester, I figured if I needed him, I could always find him at the Camlin.

I scouted around the apartment to finish up my snoop.

What I got for my efforts were more questions.

I found an embossed invitation card in a well-oiled monkey-pod bowl on the kitchen counter. It announced something called:

The Ninth Annual Bacchanalia & Moonlight Parade
An Evening of Frolic & Song
Hosted by Royce Bennington
Saturday, March 28, 1949
Festivities Begin at 7:00 P.M.
Répondez s'il vous plaît
2114—10th Avenue East—EA-4169

Royce Bennington again. This Bacchanalia was just several days away. Seemed everywhere I turned, the compass kept pointing at good old Royce Bennington.

I put the invitation into my pocket and went over the rest of the place with a fine-toothed comb. When I was done, I went over it again.

I was thumbing my way through the fancy dresses in the closet, thinking about how good Miss Jenkins would look in some of them, when I noticed what looked like the corner edge of a photo barely sticking out from behind the small dresser that I'd already gone through. I pulled the dresser away from the rear of the closet, and out fell two black & white snapshots.

The first showed a gorgeous dame jumping out of a big cake, like at a stag party or something. She wore a hot, two-piece bathing suit, had an even hotter figure, and wore her hair wavy and long.

Something about her was familiar ... By God, it was Trixie—none other than Trixie hopping out of that cake. If I hadn't seen him before, I'd of never guessed that the shapely vixen coming out of that cake was really a man. Even now, she looked so damned fetching that I could believe the stories I heard in the Marines about drunken jarheads picking up these hot dames, only to find that they had an extra package squirreled away between their legs when it came playtime.

The second photo was also of Trixie. Still in his two-piece, he was arm in arm with some joe whose face was blocked out by an idiot who'd jumped in front of the camera making the V for Victory sign. I couldn't make out his face either, as it was all blurry and out of focus.

I gave the whole apartment another once over, but came up empty. The only thing that stood out was the lack of many personal items in Trixie's digs. Normally, you'd expect to find some personal things in somebody's place— old letters, bills, a few mementoes, maybe a passbook-savings record, that kind of stuff. But not in this case. Trixie's joint contained nada of that ilk. Zip. Made me wonder if they'd been carted off by whoever preceded me in tearing the place apart. Also made me wonder about old Chucky-boy who had said he was just here to get some personal items.

I decided to get on the horn to Miss Jenkins. If I could get some help, I'd feel better about taking the time off for my belated birthday dinner tonight.

Luckily, Trixie's phone was still working, so I spun the dial for the office. Miss Jenkins picked right up on the second ring like she had in the good old days when she was still just my girl Friday.

"Rossiter Agency," she answered, pleasant as punch.

"Miss Jenkins. Glad you're there. Listen, I—"

"Where are you?"

"I'm over at Trixie's apartment. I found some dope that's pretty interesting. That's why—"

"I told you I made reservations for us again tonight," she said, curtly. "Top O' the Town. Six o'clock sharp."

"Can I talk now, Miss Jenkins? Perchance tell you what I called to tell you?"

"Only if it doesn't interfere with our dinner," she huffed.

I ignored her remark. "Look, where are you with the A-1 Bail Bond case? Got it wrapped up?"

"Better than wrapped up," Miss Jenkins said. "*Paid*. I've got a fat check in my hand as we speak. Ten percent of Blinky's skipped bail."

"Good."

"Better than good," she told me. "As a matter of fact, Louie was so happy with my work that he wants to hire me full time. At twice my current salary, I might add."

"Sure."

"Really."

"You're pulling my leg."

"Well, only a little." She laughed, sounding more like her usual self. "At least Louie said that *he'd* certainly never miss dinner with me."

"Louie never misses dinner with anybody. That's why he weighs four hundred pounds."

"He's nice, though," she said.

"Until you skip out on him," I told her. "Anyway, good job. Say, you hear anything from Heine?"

"No. Nothing today. Nothing yesterday, either."

"Not like him not to check in," I said.

"I know he's been awfully busy with the Horowitz case."

"Yeah, I know. Nothing to worry about," I said, even though I *was* worried—a little pissed, too.

"What do you need him for?" she asked.

"Same thing I need you for. This business with Trixie is getting complicated," I said. "You have anything else on the burner right now?"

"Not at the moment. What's going on?"

"Too much to explain over the phone," I told her. "I want you to pop right down to the Garden of Allah."

"Again? What for?"

"Question the patrons. Sweettalk anybody who was there last night. See if they saw or heard anything that we don't know about. Also, if Martin's there, I want you to get his story again. Start to finish. I want to compare it to what he told me yesterday, see if there are any inconsistencies."

"Don't you trust him?"

"Way this is shaping up, I don't trust anybody."

"Well, O.K.," she said. "But where will you be? Those reservations are for six o'clock. If you care about me at all, you won't miss—"

"Don't worry," I told her. "I'll meet up with you at the Garden in about an hour. Meantime, I'm going to pay a surprise visit to Donny and Martin's house. Most folks on the lam don't stray too far from home. It'd be just our luck that Donny's been hiding out right under our noses. Oh, and leave a message for Heine before you head out. Tell him to get hold of me. Dollars to donuts we're going to need him."

"Roger," said Miss Jenkins. "I'll leave the message with the answering service right away, then get changed."

"Changed?" I said. "What're you talking about?"

"Changed into my dinner dress," she said, like I was an idiot for asking. "What do you think? We're going out to eat and dance. I brought my ensemble with me just in case I didn't have time to go home and change for dinner."

"Oh … Pardon me for asking."

"How about you?" she ventured. "You better have time to change before we go out."

"Relax. I'll be dressed to the nines."

"Better be. This is special."

"So you've been telling me," I said. "Look, we're wasting time. I'll meet you later at the Garden. Out."

I hung up before she had a chance to rattle on about my attire any further. True, my suit was little rumpled from all I'd put it through, but I had more important things to worry about than being the nattiest joe at the dinner table.

Even so, I did stop at a cleaners and asked them to press the snap back into my blue suit. Then, with a tank full of ethyl and my foot to the accelerator, I headed up the long, steep slope that led to the top of Queen Anne Hill.

I found it ironic that Donny and Martin lived right across the street from Kinnear Park, which was notorious as a place for Nancy-boys pulling public indecencies in the men's john.

Nobody answered the door at their big, brick colonial. Not the front door, nor the side door, nor the back door. The place was quiet as the lovely tree-lined boulevard at the edge of the bluff that overlooked Elliott Bay, its sweeping view broken only by a few graceful Madrona trees. I tried the front door another time, but heard only the repeating sounds of the door chimes and the keening gulls riding the currents just past the bluff.

Not willing to take no for an answer, I stole around back and used my skeletons keys on the rear door. My point of entry led into an extra-large kitchen—country kitchens, they were calling them these days. It was bigger than most living rooms, had a quality red tile floor, and was appointed with all the latest in appliances and gadgets. It was also spotless. So clean and spotless, in fact, that one thing stuck out like a sore thumb: the big box of Post Toasties and half-eaten bowl of cereal that sat on the table in the knotty pine breakfast nook built into the kitchen's far corner.

I walked over and felt the cereal bowl. The milk was still cold.

Chapter

7

LISTENING FOR ANY SOUND, I MOVED quietly through the swinging door that led out to a huge dining room. A quick glance told me that it was empty, except for containing about half of the best French Provincial furniture on the planet.

Slipping under the ornately carved, fruitwood archway into the living room, I found the other half of the planet's best French Provincial furniture, as well as most of Persia's finest carpets. The living room, about the size of Memorial Stadium, contained enough ultra high-end stuff to provide any dozen fences comfortable retirements. Man, Donny and Martin didn't just live high on the hog, it looked like they could afford to buy the whole state of Iowa. I knew Donnie was rich, but brother, the place was full of expensive knick-knacks, fine oil paintings, and chintz drapes and such right up the old ying-yang. The living room's entire back wall was lined with posh, glass-fronted curio cabinets—ten of them, to be exact—all in a row like you might find at some nice museum. Each of the cabinets was chock-full of an assortment of different boxes, some large, some small, and every size in between.

I went over and examined them more closely. Some of the boxes were made of carved wood; some were gilded; some had miniature paintings on them; others were either made of plain, polished wood or of various buffed metals: gold, silver, pewter, etc.

Curious, I cracked the door to one of the cabinets and took out a small box. It was heavier than I expected, only about six inches square and four inches tall. I opened its hinged top and was surprised as hell when it loudly played *Brahm's Lullaby*.

I snapped it closed as fast as I could. Hoped the damned thing hadn't given away my presence to anybody who might be in the house. I held position and listened intently for a long moment. Heard only silence.

So, Donny and Martin collected music boxes. Must have been close to three or four hundred of them in all the curio cabinets. Strange thing for grown men to collect. Then again, they were certainly less dangerous than Royce Bennington's gun and knife collections.

I was just making my way to the wide staircase by the main entry, when I heard a noise coming from upstairs. Sounded like somebody crying. I crept up the stairs.

It was crying, all right. The sound of a man sobbing coming from the second door down the hallway ahead of me. I went to the door and pulled it open. There, sitting on a big, four-poster bed, and wearing a tuxedo that looked like he'd slept in it, was Donny, crying his eyes out.

He didn't notice me until I stepped into the bedroom and said, "Hey, you're only wanted for murder—it's not as bad as all that."

He jumped—shook the bed as he looked up at me—his

eyes all red and his sinuses all snotty. "Rossiter!" he yelped. "How did you find me?"

"Decided to look under my nose," I told him. "What's all the blubbering about?"

"Never mind," he said, taking out his handkerchief and drying his eyes.

"O.K. How about question number two, then," I said, pulling out a Philip Morris. "Why'd you rabbit?"

"I couldn't go to jail," he said anxiously, then blew his nose. "I've been there before . . . I just couldn't."

"Martin and I sure did."

"I'm sorry . . . I'm sorry."

I fired up my smoke. "You're going to have to turn yourself in, Donny."

"No! I can't." He fidgeted like a squirrel caught between two dogs.

"*You will*," I stated.

"You don't know what they do to people like us in jail."

"But first," I continued, "I've got a couple more questions for you." I looked him square in the eye. "Numero uno: did you kill Trixie?"

"No. Absolutely, I did not. Why would I? We just signed her to a six-month contract."

"O.K." I took a deep drag off my smoke. I'd seen a lot of people lie in my time, but at the moment Donny didn't seem to be one of them. "Try this on for size: what happened last night when Trixie got murdered? I got Martin's version of the story. Now, I want yours. And I want it in detail."

"Well," he said, nervously nibbling at his lower lip. "I'd just gotten—"

But that was as far as he got. At that exact moment, half the damned police force came busting into the bedroom.

"Hands up!" they shouted, their service revolvers drawn and ready for action.

Back in the same cell that Martin and I had occupied last night. It wasn't a good feeling. But it was worse for Donny. The cops had given him a real going over. Had no reason to pound on him. Which was always enough reason for them.

Donny sat on the bunk across from me. He had a knot on his forehead the size of a fifty-cent piece and a split lip. His left eye was all blue-purple and was swollen completely shut.

"You took one hell of a beating, Donny."

"Yes," he said quietly. "I've had worse."

"You're a tough little nut, aren't you?"

He smiled, albeit a bit wanly.

He was pretty brave. Had more guts than most. Reminded me of a few of the little guys I met during the war. Pint-sized runts you thought would never make it, but turned into ruthless, screaming banshees when the chips were down.

"They have the jail quack look at that eye?" I asked him.

"Of course not."

"Well," I said, getting to my feet. "You need to put something on it. Get that swelling down."

"Like what?"

"A nice beefsteak would be good," I said, moving in and examining the damage more closely. "But, since the icebox seems empty at the moment, we'll have to improvise."

I took the handkerchief out of my pocket, got it unfolded, then headed for the tankless, single toilet at the rear of the cell.

"What are you doing?" Donny asked.

I flushed the toilet, then dipped my handkerchief into the fresh water that filled the bowl.

"Good God," said Donny, behind me. "You're not … "

His voice trailed off as I squeezed most of the water out of the handkerchief. I crossed back to him with it. "Here, put this on your eye."

He drew back. "I'm not putting that anywhere near my face. Not in a million years."

"Nice cold poultice. Best we've got."

He batted my hand away. "Keep it."

"The water's clean," I said, offering it again.

"Stay away from me. It's disgusting."

I knelt down in front of him. "Look, pal. I've seen some fighters in the ring lose their sight from blimped up eyes like yours if they didn't get them treated right. And I mean *permanently*."

"No … "

"*Yes*." I held the dripping handkerchief right up to his face. "Now put this on your damned eye or you could end up wearing a patch for the rest of your life."

He thought about it for a moment.

"*Do it*."

He hesitantly took the handkerchief, then held it against his bad eye. A thin trickle of water immediately came out of it and ran down his cheek straight into the corner of his mouth. "Ugh," he muttered, wiping it away with his free hand. "This is awful … Just awful … "

"Keep it there. I'll freshen it up with more cold water in a minute."

"Oh, thanks. That'll just be the cat's pajamas."

I suddenly got a sinking feeling in the pit of my stomach. I checked my Bulova: almost 6:00! Sonofabitch. If I didn't

72

get hold of Miss Jenkins, she was likely to treat me worse than the cops.

I marched to the cell door and rattled the bars. "Guard! Guard!" I yelled. No response. "Hey, Mahoney!" I hollered, loud as I could. "You working tonight? I want my phone call, you hear me? You owe me one phone call and I want it now!"

I kept shaking the bars and repeating myself until I heard a door open somewhere up the long hallway.

"What's all the ruckus back there?"

"Give me my phone call—right now!" I shouted.

"That you making all that noise, Rossiter?" The voice came nearer, accompanied by what sounded like keys clanking together.

"Damned right! Let me out of here; I need to get on the horn."

Mahoney came into view on the other side of the bars, his big key ring held in his left hand. Didn't say anything. Just stared at me. Then at Donny.

"Open up," I told him.

He cracked a grin. "You really get around, don't you Rossiter? Different date every night."

"Very funny."

"Never thought you were the type." He laughed at his own dim wit. "Oh, well, guess it takes all kinds."

"You're a regular Bob Hope," I told him.

"O.K.," he said, turning all serious. "Step back from the cell door." I did as ordered.

He put the handcuffs on me and I scrammed out of the cell while the going was good. Mahoney led me up the corridor and got the steel door at the end unlocked.

Just as he pulled it open, a gruff voice rang out from

the main cellblock down the hall to the right. "That you, screw?"

Mahoney ignored the man. Just motioned me through the door.

"What'cha doin', screw?" the man yelled. "Takin' another Nancy-boy out for a test drive?"

"Shuttup, you!" Mahoney hollered.

He was answered by a burst of laughter from the main cells. Beet red, he followed me through the door, then slammed it like an earthquake behind him.

Much as I liked Mahoney getting a taste of his own medicine, I kept it to myself. I needed the phone more than I needed to wisecrack at the moment.

"There's the phones," he told me. "Make your call and make it snappy," he added, pointing at the bank of three pay phones set against the far wall of the linoleum-floored room that doubled as waiting area and guard station. He went over to his desk, dug a nickel out of its top drawer, and handed it to me. Then he returned to the desk, sat down, and turned on his table model radio.

" … 'America has no place for Communists, their sympathizers, and other undesirables,' said FBI Director, J. Edgar Hoover … "

That's all the news I overheard, as getting the nickel into the slot was a little tough while still handcuffed. I fiddled with it for a while, but finally managed to drop it in. Holding the phone and dialing at the same time was impossible, however. Hoping I'd remembered the number correctly, I let the receiver dangle by its cord while I dialed, then got a two-handed hold on it again as the phone began to ring.

"Garden of Allah," answered a male voice on the other end of the line.

"Listen," I said. "You've got a young woman there that I need to reach. It's important. Her name's Jenkins. About five-foot-three, slim and pretty, curly strawberry-blonde hair. You spot her anywhere?"

"Sure, bud," said the man. "You're in luck." He was momentarily drowned out by a bunch of applause in the background. "Sorry about that," he said. "We've got Mitzy Morgan just coming to the microphone."

"Great. How about Miss Jenkins? Can you put her on the line?"

There was a small clunk as he set the phone down, followed by more applause, and a sultry-voiced singer launching into, "I'm In The Mood For Love," accompanied by a smooth organ.

"Hello?" Miss Jenkins said, at length.

"Got trouble, doll," I told her.

"What? What kind of trouble? Where are you? Do you know what time it is?"

"Jail," I said. "And it's time to get me out of here."

"What? Again?"

"You heard me. Dammit, I'm sorry, but I got scooped up with Donny over at his place."

"You're with Donny? They caught him?"

"Right on both counts."

"In jail?"

"That's what I said."

She was quiet a minute. The only thing I could hear was Mitzy doing a few more bars of "I'm In The Mood For Love." Finally, Miss Jenkins said, "*I don't believe this.*"

"Look, just wait there for me. I'll make it up to you."

"Sure."

"Hey, I'm pissed about this myself. You think it's fun being stuck in the hoosegow again? Just get me out of here."

"How am I supposed to do that?" she sniffed. "The courts are all closed by now. Can't you call somebody?"

"Used my one and only call on you, kiddo. Get cracking. Spin the dial for Lt. Baker. He'll get me sprung."

"Roger," she said. "I'll try to reach him."

"O.K.," I said. "You find anything out there at the Garden?"

"Well, I talked to five different people and got five different stories about what happened. I don't know if—"

"All right, Rossiter!" Mahoney's voice boomed out behind me. "Time's up! You've had your call. Get off the line and back to lock-up."

"Who on earth is that?" asked Miss Jenkins.

"The *concierge*," I told her. "He's about as classy as his joint."

"Hang it up!"

"Gotta go, doll. Get Baker." I put the phone back in its cradle, and told Mahoney, "You know, you're about as rude as some telephone operators."

"Let's go," he said. "The Lone Ranger's coming on in a couple minutes, and I ain't missing him and Tonto."

Donny was dipping my handkerchief into the toilet when Mahoney deposited me, then vamoosed back to his radio.

"Helps, doesn't it?" I asked.

"Once you get used to it," he said, squeezing it out and putting it back on his bad eye. "Did you reach Miss Jenkins?"

"Yeah." I sat on my bunk and fired up a fag. "Thanks."

"And?" Donny asked, taking a seat on his own bunk across from me.

"She's going to try to spring me. You, on the other hand, are in a jam. Anything you haven't told me, you better spill for your own good."

"I've told you everything."

"Not really," I said. "I got the story about Trixie's murder, such as it is, from Martin, not you. How about you spin me your own narrative? Take it from the top."

"Well," he said, readjusting the wet handkerchief, which still dripped down his face no matter which way he held it. "Martin was out front with the crowd, and I was backstage with Trixie. She'd barely gotten dressed in time for me to announce her act. Then I noticed the seam of her gown splitting out under her arm. She couldn't on like that. I sent her back to her dressing room for another gown, and said I'd announce a slight delay. Just as I was going out front, two guys tried to get backstage, and I told them to get out, they weren't allowed, and—"

"What guys?"

"Two men I hadn't seen before."

"You'd never met them?"

"No. But that isn't unusual. We get a lot of folks from out of town sometimes. Word gets around. Seattle's become a real destination spot. Especially with folks from small towns and such. They don't have anything like the Garden where a lot of them live. Poor folks, a lot of them don't have anything at all, in fact. Sad. Sad, lonely lives. You can always tell those people when they come in. It's almost like they've found a family for the first time."

"O.K. What happened next?"

Donny thought for a minute. Actually scratched his head then said, "Oh, yes ... I shooed them back to their table, then went to the microphone to make the announcement about

77

Trixie's act being delayed for a few minutes. That's when the argument started."

"Argument?"

"Yes. Between Big Bill and this sailor. The swabby was over at their table bothering her partner, Little Bill."

"Who's this Big Bill and Little Bill?" I asked.

"They live at the YWCA—they're a couple. Big Bill's tough as they come, rides a motorcycle with the Motor Maids of America. Anyway, she doesn't like anybody making eyes at Little Bill. I knew there was going to be trouble. I tried to go over and break it up, but before I went six feet, Big Bill came up out of her chair and decked that sailor. Boy, is she rough. One punch and it was lights out for the Navy. Then I heard the scream."

"Trixie?"

"Yes." He slowly shook his head. "It wasn't all that loud, actually. At first, I thought it was just somebody in the crowd, what with the ruckus between Big Bill and the sailor. Then I heard it again. Kind of faint and distant. It came from backstage. That's when I ran back, and we found poor Trixie in her dressing room. God, she was covered with blood... So much blood... It was awful."

"Was he already dead when you got to him?"

Donny didn't speak. Just nodded his head, *yes*.

"Anybody else around?"

"No."

"Think carefully," I told him. "This is important." I stubbed my butt out on the floor. "Did you see anybody at all? How about just in the general vicinity backstage?"

"No, I told you," Donny said. "I didn't see anybody."

"You sure?"

"Yes, for God's sake. How many times do I have to tell you?"

"O.K. Take it easy," I said.

Donny was all agitated. Got up off his bunk and paced back and forth in front of the cell door like the wolves and coyotes you see at the zoo. "What am I going to do?" he said. "What am I going to do?"

"Hey, like I told you, take it easy. It'll work out."

"No. It's not that."

"What is it?"

His eyes filled with tears. "I think Martin's been cheating on me!"

Chapter

8

"THAT'S INTERESTING," I SAID. "MARTIN thinks you've been cheating on *him*."

"I know—I know," said Donny. "He must be trying to teach me a lesson. It's over between us. I just know it is."

"Well, my condolences," I told him. "But you two can work on your relationship on your own time. Right now, let's stick to Trixie. Who would want to kill him?"

Took Donny a minute to calm himself down, then he said, "Trixie was a user and a taker. She had quite a temper, too. She'd flare up and do stupid things."

"What?" I asked. "That's not what Martin told me. According to him, Trixie was as pure as the driven snow."

"Sure," said Donny. "When she wanted something."

"Boy, you and Martin really tend to contradict each other," I said.

"I'm sure any number of people aren't unhappy that Trixie's gone," he continued. "But as to anybody wanting to kill her, well, I can't imagine somebody going that far."

"Somebody did."

"Yes," he said softly. "Well, I don't know anymore about it than I've told you."

"O.K., we'll change the topic for now," I told him. "How

about this? Anybody putting the squeeze to you down at the club?"

"Aside from the cops, you mean?" he asked. "Yes. Rollo Mudd."

"Rollo Mudd?" I asked, a little taken aback at the mention of his name. Rollo was serious business. One of our fair burg's biggest racket-kings, I'd never had a personal run-in with Mr. Mudd, and had always been content to leave it that way.

"How did Rollo Mudd ever get his hooks into you, Donny?"

"Oh, it was pretty simple, actually," he said. A fleeting smile crossed his lips. "His collector, Dennis Diamond came to the show one night, said how much he liked it, then told us how much it was going to cost us to keep putting it on."

"Dennis Diamond, huh?" I whistled. "Tough customer from all I've heard. How long's this been going on?"

"About a year," Donny told me. "Diamond comes in once a week for the payoff. I wish they'd send somebody else. He gives me the creeps."

"I don't imagine."

"No, it's not that," Donny said, repositioning the compress on his eye. "He's truly creepy. Really hinky. Always bothering our female impersonators."

"Yeah? How so?"

"He usually stays awhile when he comes in. Always takes a table right up front and makes a big deal out of ogling all our impersonators. If they're doing a torch song, he yells, "oh, baby," and "yeah, baby … that's it, baby!" at the top of his lungs. He'll even bend down low and pretend like he's looking up their skirts." Donny gave a slight shudder. "He's just so vulgar and rude. The girls tolerated him because he was a big tipper. But Trixie hated him. She thought it was disrespectful."

"Hassled Trixie, too, huh?"

"Way more than most," said Donny. "Diamond seemed particularly taken with Trixie. He'd act up even more than usual around her. He even shot rubber bands at her one time. She gave him a good slap."

"Slapped Dennis Diamond?"

"That's the funny thing," said Donny. "Diamond didn't do anything. He just stood there and took it. Didn't raise a finger to her."

"No kidding."

"Yes. He just rubbed at his cheek for a moment. Then he smiled, of all things, and left the club without so much as saying a word—forgot to collect the payoff."

"Strange," I said. "How long ago was that?"

"Just last week."

I got to my feet, now particularly interested in Mr. Dennis Diamond. "Was Diamond at the club the night Trixie got killed?"

"No. He hasn't been in since she slapped him."

"You're sure about that."

"Yes."

"O.K.," I said. "Just out of curiosity, where's Rollo Mudd holding court these days? I might just have to pay him a visit. Last I heard he was operating out of the Kool Kat Club."

"No, that's closed down, now. Out of business. Diamond told me Mudd has a new set-up at Club Rialto."

"Club Rialto, huh? That figures," I said, thinking about the city's biggest strip joint. I hadn't been in the place since Bubbles LaFlamme got killed. Kind of soured me on burlesque. "Owners must be into old Rollo pretty deep."

"Deeper than deep, from what Diamond told me. Mudd's taken it over. He's running the place now."

"Well, how about that?" I said.

We were interrupted by the sound of the main cell-block door clanking open up the corridor. "Hey, Rossiter!" came Mahoney's bellowing voice. "Pack it up and move it out! You're getting sprung!" More than one set of footsteps echoed down the hallway toward me.

"What?" I yelled back, grabbing hold of our cell door's bars and straining to see who was with Mahoney.

The answer to my question popped into view in short order: Lieutenant Baker, one of the few cops I was ever glad to see.

"Pays to have a little extra juice, doesn't it, Jake?" he said, as Mahoney, not looking too happy, slid his key into the door lock. "I'm getting you out of here. And put a rush on it: I'm late for a Pinochle party with my girlfriend."

I stepped out of the cell as fast as I could.

"Hey," said Donny. "What about me?"

"We'll get to you in the morning," Baker told him.

"I didn't do anything."

"Call your lawyer," said Baker. "Let's go, Jake."

As we started up the hall, Donny said, "Shit. Shit." If he said anymore, I didn't hear it, as I quickened my pace and got the hell out of there in more than a hurry to pick up my personal effects and try to meet up with Miss Jenkins.

My .45 firmly in its holster, I bid adieu to Mahoney and made like a bunny out of city jail. Baker and I paused a moment on the front steps as I took in a deep breath of free, crisp air.

That's when the flashbulbs started popping. Between the loud pops and bright flashes, I almost went for my gun. Then

I recognized the source, positioned on the sidewalk at the bottom of the stairs: none other than sleazy Blaine Conway, damned pesty police beat reporter for the *Seattle Star*, and his blasted photographer, who was slapping in fresh flashbulbs as fast as he could.

"Rossiter!" hollered the hack, wisely keeping his distance. "Care to comment on you being arrested in the company of a known homosexual? For the second time in two days, no less!"

"Fuck you, Conway!" I yelled, and started to go for him.

Baker held me back. "Get hold of yourself, man."

"What's your involvement with the notorious Garden of Allah and the murder of this female impersonator?" asked Conway, with a leer and obvious relish. Two more quick flashes. "Were you part of some sordid homosexual love triangle?"

That tore it. I broke away from Baker and rushed down the steps.

A black sedan pulled up. They quickly backed toward it, the photog snapping yet another picture of me, as somebody inside the car pushed open the rear door for them. I was only six feet away, when they hopped inside and the sedan sped off, Conway's head sticking out the window and screaming back at me, "Read all about it in the morning *Star*, Rossiter!"

The car squealed out of sight down the block.

"Sonofabitch!" I threw my fedora to the pavement.

"You can say that again," said Baker, catching up to me. "I think they got me in some of those pictures with you."

"Is that all you're worried about?" I asked, the fresh night air now smelling more than foul. I picked up my hat and smoothed it out. "You afraid you'll be tainted by asscociating with me?"

"Hell, no," he said, fishing out his pack of Old Golds. "On the other hand, damned yellow journalists, I wouldn't put it past them. Sonofabitch. And I'm up for promotion."

I lit one of my own smokes, and kicked at the pavement, even though there was nothing on it to kick at. "How in Sam Hill did they know to be here like that?" I asked.

"Didn't come from me," he said. "I blew out in a rush when Miss Jenkins called. They must have followed me. Reporter's room is just at the end of the hall down from my office."

"Great." My cigarette tasted off. "Fuck it."

"Yeah, fuck it," he said. "Just fuck it."

"Well, thanks for springing me, but I've got places to be."

"Same-same," said Baker. "Need a lift?"

"Yeah, make it snappy."

Baker dropped me and took off to his card party, and I beat feet for the Garden of Allah to meet up with Miss Jenkins at last.

Turned out I went on a fool's errand. Recent murder or not, the Garden was hopping. *Without Miss Jenkins in attendance.* I couldn't find her at all. Her nor Martin, either.

Finally, I went up to the trim joe tending bar and asked about Miss Jenkins.

"Oh, yes," he said. "She left a note with me for you."

"Gimmee," I said.

He handed it over—small note written on a page from her pocket notebook. It was brief and to the point:

> *Jake,*
> *Tired of waiting. Got invited to a party with a nice girl I met named Dolores. Maybe we can try again tomorrow night for your birthday. I made reservations for 6:00 again.*

85

It won't be the same, but third time's a charm, so they say.
It remains to be seen.
 Have a nice night.

Damn, I thought, *damn*. "You have any idea where they went?" I asked the bartender.

"Beats me," he said.

"This girl, Dorlores. You know her?"

"Sure. She comes in now and then."

"She's not a *he* is she?"

"No."

"Does she like girls?"

"She's got a boyfriend, mac."

"Thanks," I told him. "By the way, where's Martin?"

"Out and about, I guess," he said. "Haven't seen him since I came on duty."

"Great."

I left. Stood out on the sidewalk for a minute smoking another cigarette that tasted off. What a fine kettle of fish this was. What the hell—she could have waited for me a little longer—I wasn't that late.

I caught a cab up to Donny's place and picked up the Roadmaster. Then I spun by the office and found it empty. I tried the answering service. No messages.

For want of anything better to do, I took myself out for a drink.

It was my only birthday present.

Chapter

9

I WOKE UP ROUGH AND LATE THE NEXT morning. Splitting head, almost 10:00, still no Miss Jenkins, and no frigging messages from Heine, to boot.

I put together equal parts of coffee, hair-of-the-dog, and Bayer aspirin.

About noon, I felt much improved, and went out. Club Rialto had a lunch show, and I figured it would be the perfect time to have a talk with Mr. Dennis Diamond.

Club Rialto hadn't changed in the last year or so. Still had the big, well-lit shadowbox by the entrance that advertised their strippers. I noted that Bunny Sunday still had top-billing, her blown-up photo filling three-quarters of the box, showing her lithe and buxom beauty in all her glory. Two other strippers had smaller photos tacked beneath hers: a raven-haired chicken named Night & Day, and some blonde with a Veronica Lake hairdo who went by the apt name of Lady Lake.

Inside, the coat check was still to the immediate right; the long bar fronted by its tall bar stools was just past that; and the tables, about thirty in all, were full of men drinking watered-down drinks. A three-piece combo accompanied the bump-and-grind on stage, which currently featured Miss

Lady Lake, already down to her gold G-string and matching, tasseled pasties.

As I passed on checking my coat and hat, Lady Lake finished her act by taking her huge bazooms in each hand and thrusting them forward at the audience, saying, "How d'ya like these, boys? *They're big and bad like Alan Ladd! Big and bad like Alan Ladd!*"

Thunderous applause and hoots and hollers. Well, I thought, she certainly made the most of her slight resemblance to Veronica Lake.

The host—same ferret-faced joe who worked here last year—came right up and offered me a table.

"Don't want a table," I told him. "I'm looking for Dennis Diamond."

"Dennis Diamond..." the host mumbled, his expression shifting into fear. "I...uh...I don't know if Mr. Diamond's here or not. He's usually in Mr. Mudd's office if he's around."

"That'll do," I said. "Where is it?"

He fidgeted. "Up the stairs by the coat check."

"Thanks." I turned and started for the stairs.

He rushed up beside me. "But you can't go up there."

"Seems that's what I'm doing."

He kept tagging along. "But I have to call Mr. Mudd, first. See if he'll see you. Please. You'll put me in a jam."

I stopped for a moment. "So, call him. You'll have done your duty, and all will be well about the time I get to his door."

I took off again. As I hit the stairway, the ferret-faced host was frantically grabbing for the phone at the coat check counter.

Top of the stairs, dead ahead, was the door marked OFFICE—

PRIVATE. If it hadn't said "Private," I might have knocked. Instead, I opened the door and walked straight in.

Rollo Mudd, seated at a large, ivory-painted desk, wearing a brown bowler hat on his head, jerked to attention as I entered. He looked pissed, but he didn't make any moves except for setting the white phone in his right hand back into its cradle. I thought he was going to ask me who I was. But he just stared bullets at me and slowly moved the gold toothpick in his mouth from side to side, as I took in the room: large for an office, powder-white walls, with thick cream-colored carpeting, two white leather chairs opposite the desk, and a matching white leather sofa sitting against the far wall next to a small ivory-colored bar with half a dozen bottles of booze sitting on it. We seemed to be alone.

I was just about to introduce myself, when I heard a toilet flush off to my right. The only other door in the room opened, and out came a brown-suited goon about the size of Mount Rainier. He started when he saw me.

"Hey! What the hell?" he barked. His right hand headed under his suit coat.

Mudd shook his head and waved him off.

Taking his hand back out from under his coat, the goon asked, "Boss, you want I should give him the bounce?"

"I bet you bounce better than I do," I told him. "Care to find out?"

The big jamoke screwed up his face and took a step toward me. Again, Mudd waved him off. Then, with a couple curls of his forefinger, Mudd beckoned his man over, and quietly spoke in his ear.

"Boss wants to know who you are," the goon told me.

"Name's Rossiter. Jake Rossiter."

The lug bent his ear again, then popped back up with another question. "Heat?"

"Private," I said. "Something wrong with Mr. Mudd's voice or what?"

"Boss don't talk to just anybody." He bent his ear again. "What d'ya want?"

"Dennis Diamond. Like to ask him a few questions."

Again with the down and up.

"Boss says questions cost money."

"What, he wants me to pay him?"

"That's the drift. Time is money. You're takin' his time."

I laughed.

They didn't.

"O.K.," I said. "I'll play along. Maybe once. How much?"

"Sawbuck for starters."

I dug one out of my wallet and handed it over. Couldn't believe I was getting held up by this hood just to ask a few questions. "There. Where can I find Dennis Diamond?"

"Ain't here," said Mudd's lug. "What d'ya want with him?"

"Questions cost money," I said, throwing them my best shit-eating grin.

"What?" the big man exclaimed. "You tryin' to hold up the boss, you wiseacre?"

"Two can play at this game," I said. "Answer'll cost you a sawbuck."

Rollo Mudd exploded with laughter. His goon looked at him like he was nuts, but Mudd just kept roaring. "I like this joe!" he told his man. "You got real wit, Rossiter," he said, standing up and taking the gold toothpick out of his mouth. "Balls to match. How about a drink?"

He didn't wait for my answer. Just adjusted his bowler to

a jaunty angle, stepped out from behind his desk and made straight for the bar, walking with the swagger of a man who was on top of the world.

"You like bourbon, Mr. Rossiter?" he asked, picking up a bottle of bourbon. "No matter. You have a bourbon with me." He poured two quick shots, handed me one, then sat back at his desk. "Sit down. Take a load off," he told me.

I kept to my feet.

"So," Mudd said, tossing off his shot. "What d'ya want with my man, Diamond?"

"Questions, like I said. I understand he collects for you at the Garden of Allah."

Mudd's expression went suddenly cold. "What d'ya know about my business?"

"Just enough to keep out of it," I told him.

He smiled again. "Yeah, that's smart."

"If I can."

Mudd frowned, then gave me a wry smile. "You're a cagey dick, aren't you? O.K., Diamond's my boy. My right-hand boy. Helps me out all over town. Truth is, I don't know where Dennis is right now. I gave him a couple days vacation. He ain't been himself of late. Off. You know what I mean? He's been a little off. You know anything about that?"

"Confidential," I said.

He laughed. "Confidential, huh? You barge in here asking about my best boy, then you tell me it's confidential. This got something to do with that broad of his?"

"Which one is that?"

"The one what skipped out on him last week; who else?"

"Could be," I said.

"Fucking broads," said Mudd. He stalked to the bar and poured himself another bourbon. "Nothing but trouble.

91

Been my boy's main squeeze for over two years, then she disappears. Get a new dame, I tell him. It's easier. But no, he wants her. He's been scouring the town for her and neglecting his work."

Mudd suddenly walked up to me, stood eyeball to eyeball. "What you're working on, dick," he said, "will it fuck with Diamond?"

"No," I said, with a straight face.

"It fucks with Diamond, it fucks with my business," he told me, his eyes as mean as a Doberman's.

"I said, no."

"Good. I'll take your word for it." He kept staring into my eyes. I didn't blink. He smiled. "Got a little proposition for ya, then."

"What's that?"

"I want you to find Diamond's dame."

I didn't respond.

"Why so quiet?" Mudd asked. "You holding something back on me?"

"No," I said. "I was just wondering what's in it for me."

"I'll pay ya. More than worth it. I got a business to run. Pay you a fat bonus if you find her quick. Need my boy back on form. What d'ya say?"

"I'm going to need some details, some background," I told him. "On her and Dennis Diamond both."

"You'll get everything you need," said Mudd. He went back to his desk and pulled out his checkbook. "For starters, you'll get this check for three hundred. Sammy there," he said, gesturing at his man, "will fill you in on all the info you need. And just remember: you don't stay on the square, I'll fill you in with everything you need, too." He pulled a big automatic out of his desk drawer and held it up for me to see. "And that includes all eight pieces of lead in this pistol. Get my drift?"

"Unmistakably," I said. "Diamond and his broad, they live together or keep separate pads?"

"Together," Mudd said, finishing out the check.

Sammy spoke up. "I'll give ya all the info."

"I'll need an address."

"You'll get it."

"Here." Mudd handed me the check.

I folded it into my inside pocket. "Oh, by the way, her name would help. What is it?"

"Dolores," said Mudd. "Dolores Carver. She's a seamstress. Makes dresses or something."

Chapter

10

MISS JENKINS SEEMED A BIT OFF. INSTEAD of her usual smile, she frowned at me when I came in.

"You mad about me missing dinner last night?" I asked.

"More like *very* disappointed," she said, staring icicles at me for a moment. "But I don't feel quite up to yelling at you just now." She pulled her compact out of her purse and took a gander at herself in its little mirror. "Darn." She fussed with her face for a second, and repeated, "Darn." Snapping the compact closed with an audible click, she said, "Anyway, that darned party was just too much fun."

"Hangover?"

"Well, now that you mention it, I do have a hangover— just a tad."

"Yeah? Gee, I'd hate to see the real McCoy."

"Do I look that bad?"

"How do you feel?"

"Not good."

"There's your answer," I told her. "Miss Jenkins, what you need is a little hair-of-the-dog. You sit tight, and I'll get you some. Then you can tell me all about this party over your pick-me-up. I'm more than interested."

"Oh, I don't know if I could drink anymore," she said. "I'm—"

"Good for what ails you." Heading for my office, I added, "Trust me."

I returned in short order with my bottle of Cutty Sark and a water tumbler, into which I sloshed a few fingers and handed over to my junior partner. Then I took a seat opposite her desk.

She tentatively brought the glass to her lips, then made a sour face as the full bouquet of the peaty malt wafted up at her.

"Down the hatch," I said. "Hold your nose if you have to."

She actually did hold her nose, and managed to get a good gulp down. With a slight shudder, she asked, "What—you're not having any?"

"Pass."

"You always drink."

"Not this time around," I told her. "My stomach's started feeling a little off, for some reason. Finish your medicine."

Much to my surprise, she quaffed the last of her Scotch like a good patient.

"Feel better?"

"No."

"You will." I fired up a smoke. "So, tell me about this party. Where was it?"

"At Royce Bennington's house."

"Royce Bennington? It was at *his* place?"

"Yes. Anything wrong with that?"

"Maybe plenty."

"Not that I could see. In fact, it was swell." She leaned back in her chair and had a good stretch. "Golly, I've never been in a place like that before. It was like a palace."

"It *is* a palace," I told her. "That's how the other half lives, doll. No, strike that," I corrected myself. "Actually, that's how the other *less than one percent* lives. Anyway, go on. Sounds like the rich snake threw quite a bash. I want to hear all about it."

"Snake?" she asked, leaning across the desk at me. "Why would you say that? I know you went over there. Did you had some sort of run-in with him?"

"Just a minor one. Good chance there'll be more to come."

"Well, he was a perfect gentleman with me. And a wonderful host. And that fancy smoking room of his with the hookah. Boy, what a place."

"You went to his smoking room?" I felt my blood doing a slow boil.

"Yes," she said. "Why not?"

"You didn't smoke anything did you?"

"Well, of course I smoked. At least I think I did." She paused, looked a little confused. "It was later in the evening. I remember that Royce insisted I try it and—"

"Insisted, huh?"

"Oh, well, I had a whole lot of fun, anyway," she said. "Royce has parties most every night. He had a jillion guests there, but he took the time to show me all around. And the food—there was prime rib and king crab and baked ham and buckets and buckets of caviar—he even had a huge fountain that was bubbling with champagne. Real champagne. You just went over and filled your glass right from it. As many times as you wanted. Boy, I liked that."

"Obviously."

She ignored my jibe and continued. "And the men, gosh, I've never seen so many well dressed, handsome men in my life. Scads of them. If you don't mind me saying so, they were just drop-dead gorgeous."

"Lots of wolves, huh?"

"Wolves? Hardly. No, all the men were of a different persuasion, I think."

"Oh … Should've known. Must have been a bit uncomfortable."

"No. *It was wonderful!*" she blurted.

"Excuse me?"

"No wolves," she said, as if that explained anything. "Could I have some more Scotch? You're right: it is making me feel a little better." I poured her another finger, and she sipped at it as she continued. "There weren't any wolves, don't you get it? Well, I guess I wouldn't have either, since I'd never been to a party like this before. Look, here's what I mean: there I was, surrounded by tons of men, but nobody was pawing at me. Not one of them tried to make time with me. It was odd, at first, but then I felt completely relaxed. I could just enjoy myself without any worries. It was *positively liberating.*"

I couldn't help thinking that if I was surrounded by bevies of beautiful broads, but not one of them was amenable to my charms, it wouldn't be liberating at all—it would be *positively devastating.*

"How did you find out about this party, anyway?" I asked.

"From Dolores."

"Dolores?"

"Yes. That's the girl I went with."

"She mention a boyfriend?"

"No."

"You sure?"

"Yes. What are you on about?"

"How about what she does for a living? She mention that?"

"As a matter of fact, she did. She's a seamstress and dress designer. She makes all the gowns for all the guys at the Garden of Allah. Can you believe it? Isn't that—"

"You need to stay away from this woman." I got to my feet. "Understand?"

"What?" She also stood up. "Why would you say that? She was a whole lot of fun and—"

"She's got a dangerous boyfriend."

"Dolores?"

"Name of Dennis Diamond. Tough cookie."

"How do you know about this?"

I told her about my visit with Rollo Mudd. Filled her in about him insisting on hiring me and why.

When I'd finished, Miss Jenkins sat back down. "Good grief," she said. "Poor Dolores. What a pickle. Say, you're not going to turn her over to—"

"Not for the present," I told her. "Tell you the truth, I don't know exactly what I *am* going to do. And you're right—it is a pickle—a great, big, fat kosher dill. You don't take Rollo Mudd's dough without delivering. But what I've found out about Dennis Diamond makes him as good a suspect as anybody else in Trixie's murder. I need to talk to that hoodlum. Dolores, too."

Miss Jenkins thought for a second, then said, "*I'll* talk to her."

"What?'

"Yes," she said, getting fired up to her own idea. "She knows me. She doesn't know you. And I think she trusts me. If she finds out why Rollo Mudd hired you, she'll never talk to you. And you know, women quite often know things about their boyfriends that nobody else does. Yes. I'll talk to Dolores—you talk to Dennis Diamond. Neat and simple."

"O.K." I didn't like it, but she made sense. "By the way, have you heard from Heine?"

"No. Not a word. But you did get a call from a federal judge."

"A judge? Who?"

"His name was Torrence, I think. Yes, that's it. I've got the note right here. Judge Frank Torrence."

"What's he want with me?"

"He wants you to meet him in his chambers at the Federal Courthouse tomorrow morning. Nine o'clock sharp."

"Hell's bells. What about?"

"He didn't say anything except that it's very important."

I didn't respond. Normally, I keep pretty much a poker-face about things, but I must have been letting some queasy and apprehensive feelings show, because Miss Jenkins asked, "Are you O.K.?"

"Oh, sure. Just peachy. federal judge calls you out of the blue and summons you to his chambers—who wouldn't be O.K.?"

"We haven't been working on any federal cases, have we?" she asked.

"No. Wouldn't if I had to," I told her. "You can't trust feds. I learned that the hard way back in my rum-running days. If you never have to learn that lesson first hand, doll, count it as a blessing."

"Well," she said, pulling out a piece of Blackjack gum. "Have you done anything wrong?"

"Plenty. Who hasn't?"

"That's not what I mean." She popped the gum in her mouth and chewed prodigiously. "Have you been involved with anything that the feds would be looking into?"

"Remains to be seen," I told her. "Anyway, enough of this. I'm just going to forget about it." I changed the subject. "Why don't you take the rest of the afternoon off? Our dinner-date's coming up at six. I surely won't miss it this time. You look like you could use a little rest."

"Actually, I could," she said. "Are you sure you'll be—"

"I'll be fine," I told her. "You scram. Get your beauty rest."

For once, she did as ordered. But not before insisting that she'd be doing the driving tonight. It was my birthday dinner, after all, and I should be chauffeured. She'd be back at 5:30 sharp to pick me up.

I did a piss-poor job forgetting about the judge. Finally thought I had him licked when I busied myself doing something I hardly ever did—cleaning and organizing my desk—but he stayed at the back of my mind like a four-aspirin headache.

The Top O' the Town, on the highest floor of the Sorrento Hotel, was one of the classiest restaurants in the city. Like the Cloud Room, and Canlis, it was among the absolute best that Seattle had to offer.

Beaming, Miss Jenkins led me inside like the whole place was my birthday present. I smiled back, acted like it was my first time there. I knew how much it meant to her. But I didn't put it on too heavy. I also knew that, between the expense of her fancy dress, and the cost of the meal, she'd probably be hitting me up for a raise before the month was out.

"Great spot, doll," I said, as the maître d' led us back through the linen-covered tables and white-shirted, red-sashed, oh-so-correct waiters, who bowed slightly as they took folks' orders, and seemed to have a European air to them, whether or not they'd been born in Seattle or Spokane rather than Paris or London.

Miss Jenkins had reserved a window seat. Our table faced west, with a commanding view of Elliott Bay and nearby downtown Seattle.

As the bus boy filled our crystal water glasses, Miss Jenkins sighed, and said, "*Finally*. I thought I'd never get you out here." She looked positively radiant, the forest green cocktail dress putting extra sparkles in her green-blue eyes and strawberry blonde hair.

"Me either," I told her. "Glad we made it."

"And that hangover," she said. "I thought that would louse things up again. It's amazing—I never thought I'd be able to get rid of it."

"Hair-of-the-dog," I said. "It's worked more miracles than Saint Christopher."

"Shhhh!" she scolded. "That's sacrilegious."

"So's a hangover."

"Well, there can be too much of a good thing, too." She took a sip of her water. "I must admit that I feel infinitely improved. But I've had so much hair-of-the-dog today, that I'm starting to feel a little tipsy again."

"Same-same. That's the point. You wouldn't need it if you'd behaved yourself at Bennington's little soiree."

"I *don't* want to talk about that," she snapped.

"Whoa! What'd I say?" She had a foul look on her puss. "You were fine telling me about it earlier. What's the—"

"Just never mind."

"You do something you shouldn't have?"

"Of course not."

The waiter, tall, with slicked-back black hair, showed up and asked if we'd like cocktails before the meal.

"Yes," said Miss Jenkins, "definitely." She ordered a Tom Collins. I went for a double Scotch. Neat.

After the waiter left, I thought it wise to lay off Bennington's party and changed the subject. "So," I said. "You never told me what you found out down at the Garden of Allah. You find any patrons who were there the night of Trixie's murder?"

"Some," she said, gazing out the window at the view.

"What'd they say?"

"Well, all the ones I talked to said they didn't even know that Trixie had been killed until the cops showed up."

"That figures. What else?"

"The bartender thought he heard a scream, but put it down to folks just having a good time." She fiddled with her napkin a moment—looked like she wasn't much interested in filling me in. "A woman named Big Bill said that she saw two men trying to go backstage. But they got the bum's rush from Donny."

"Yeah," I said. "I heard about that."

"Beyond that," she continued, "there wasn't much else. Most people couldn't even remember what they were doing before the police came."

The waiter arrived with our drinks, then buzzed off to another table with two long-necked Pabst Blue Ribbons on his tray.

"Such quick service." Miss Jenkins picked up her Tom Collins and smiled at me. "Let's forget business for now." She toasted me with her tall glass. "Happy, happy birthday, Jake," she said, looking deep into my eyes, her own orbs soft and warm as a summer day. I was expecting her to add something schmaltzy, but she suddenly looked past me and dropped her jaw. "Good grief…" she mumbled.

"What is it, doll?" I turned around and scanned the other side of the restaurant. Then I saw what had caused her reaction: *Heine* with some beautiful dame. Somewhere in her mid to late twenties, she was knock-out gorgeous, had wavy, long blonde locks, and wore a deep blue, low-cut evening dress that exposed a chasm of cleavage as deep as the Grand Canyon. Arm in arm like two lovebirds, she and Heine were just being seated at a window table with a southern exposure. They sat side by side, with Heine's arm wrapped around her shoulder. She gave him a big kiss on the lips, then snuggled even closer to him.

"Good grief…" Miss Jenkins repeated.

"What's wrong?"

"That's Lorna Horowitz."

"What?" I asked. "Abe Horowitz's wife? Are you sure?"

"Of course I'm sure. Mr. Horowitz showed me her picture before I put Heine on the case."

"I'll be a sonofabitch…" I stood up.

"What are you going to do?" she asked.

"What am I going to do? Heine's supposed to be getting the goods about Lorna cheating on her hubby, but he's sitting there big as life smooching her up. What do you *think* I'm going to do?"

I wheeled and made a beeline for their table.

"Jake," Miss Jenkins called after me.

I kept going. Made the sixty feet to my right-hand operative's table in no time flat, and planted myself in front of him and Lorna. Heine was just lighting her cigarette when he glanced up and noticed me.

"Hey, Jake," he said, much more nonchalantly than I thought he would. "Fancy meeting you here."

"You and me gotta talk," I told him.

"Look," he said. "Sorry I haven't called in, I—"

"*Now.*"

"O.K., O.K.—don't get all hot and bothered."

"Oh, yeah? What the hell are you doing?" I yelled. Diners nearby turned in their seats to see what was happening.

"I'm having dinner with the woman I love." He took Lorna's hand, and the biggest smile I'd ever seen crossed his heavyset mug.

"You were supposed to follow her, not date her!" I shouted, loud enough that half the restaurant began to gawk at us.

Miss Jenkins hurried to my side and grabbed my right arm. "Jake," she said, her voice quiet but tense, "you're making a scene."

"I don't care. Heine's acting like an idiot and I need to set him straight."

"Hey," Heine told me, his smile vanishing. "This is my life, Jake. Stay out of it."

"And this is *my business*," I told him. "And you're screwing it up!"

"I think we should leave," Lorna told Heine.

"Fine," he said. "We're going." They got up from the table.

"Heine, dammit—"

"Fuck you." He jabbed a thick finger at me. "Fuck you!"

I stood there a second, kind of numb.

The maître d' rushed over. "Sir," he asked me, "is there a problem?"

"No, no," explained Miss Jenkins. "There's no problem."

Before I knew it, Heine and Lorna blew by me and headed out of the joint.

"Heine!" I yelled across the restaurant.

He didn't look back. Just took her by the arm and went out the exit, Lorna throwing me a smile as they disappeared from sight.

I took a step after them, but Miss Jenkins pulled me back. "Don't you dare," she told me. "For Heaven's sake, come and sit down." She shoved me toward our table. "You've caused enough commotion."

"Who cares?"

"*Sit.*" She pushed me into my seat and re-took her own. Drumming her fingers on the table top, she gave me a dirty look. "You're being totally unprofessional."

"*Me?*"

"You have no manners." She glared at me. "Didn't your mother teach you how to behave?"

"No. I'm an orphan, remember?"

"Oh, for Pete's sake . . . "

The waiter picked just that moment to show up and ask if we were ready to order.

"Take a hike, *garçon*," I told him. "We're leaving."

"*No, we're not*," Miss Jenkins stated emphatically. The waiter held his position, glanced nervously at us. "Jake," she said, her tone softening. "We're here to celebrate your birthday."

"I'm not in the mood."

"You jerk!" she exploded, leaning across the table at me, and pounding it once for emphasis. "You big rat!"

I drew back. The waiter mumbled something and wisely left.

"Look, you." She stabbed a finger at me. "It's taken me three tries to get you out here. And now we're going to celebrate your birthday and have a nice dinner and a good time and that's *that*. Got it?"

"Hey, I—"

"*Don't* say another word."

"Miss Jenkins, I'm sorry, but I—"

"You're so selfish!" she snapped. Then she really lit into me. "Why are you always thinking about yourself? I want to spend an evening with you. That's all I want! We never get to spend any time together!"

"Of course we do. I see you in the office every day."

"That's not the same. It's work. You're always ordering me around: 'Miss Jenkins, do this—Miss Jenkins do that,' like I'm just your *junior* partner." She threw herself back in her chair and folded her arms in a huff. "I bet you don't even remember my first name."

"What do you mean by that?"

"Just what I said."

"Well, of course I remember your first name," I told her.

"Oh, yeah?" She locked eyes with me. "What is it?"

I opened my mouth, but her name wasn't there—not even on the tip of my tongue.

"Well?"

I looked around for our waiter, said, "Maybe we should order."

"My name," she said. "What is it?"

I spotted the waiter—was just about to snap my fingers for him when it came to me.

"Barbara," I told her, trying not to let my tremendous relief show. "It's Barbara."

She continued to stare me down.

"You really thought I didn't know it, didn't you?" I asked her.

"Well … " she said.

"Forget it," I told her. "Let's eat and drink and dance the

night away. Just you and me. Forget about everything else. We'll have a great time."

And that's exactly what we did, as best as I can remember. Had ourselves a grand old time. Well, if not exactly a grand time, I had as good a time as too much hooch could make it. We danced and danced some more. Danced and drank and really worked at it until the wee hours when we closed the joint down.

After that, it all gets a bit hazy. I recall getting Miss Jenkins back to her place ... Told her it was the best birthday I ever had ... Drank the nightcaps she insisted on making for us ... Even had a few good laughs ... Seem to remember her giving me a kiss ... Then, nothing. Just a big fat blank.

Think I liked that blank, too. Think I'd wanted nothing so much as a big fat blank ever since that business with Heine ...

Chapter

11

I WAS HAVING A DREAM ABOUT A BED WHEN I woke up—a wonderful dream. It was Heine and my first night in town after we'd gotten back from the war. We didn't have any place to stay yet and had splurged on a fancy room at the Olympic Hotel. What a change from the lousy jungle. The hotel room seemed like a dream in and of itself: forget how ritzy it was, and all the fancy furnishings, it had *real beds*—two twin beds with smooth cotton sheets. It was Heaven, not too hot, not too cold, just a soft mattress and a light, goose-down comforter and these sheets that felt almost better than a woman. We both slept in the next morning—no sounds of the war banging in our ears—just these slick sheets and comfy mattresses that seemed to caress you at every turn.

Like now. I rolled over on my back and stretched and felt luxurious. The sun filtering through the window was almost as pleasant as the smell of fresh-brewed coffee and—

Judas Priest! This wasn't my bedroom and this wasn't my bed and this wasn't any dream. I sat bolt upright. It was Miss Jenkins's bedroom, and I was alone in her bed *naked as a jaybird*.

I jumped out of the sack. My clothes were in a heap over by her dresser. So were Miss Jenkins's clothes—her forest-green dress, the high-heeled shoes, her nylons and garter belt, her slip, brassiere, and her...

No. No way, I thought, pulling on my trousers and stuffing my shirt into them. I'd never do that. I cared too much for her. Wouldn't happen. I wouldn't let it. And neither would she. Something like that, especially with her, I'd sure as hell remember it.

Where the devil was she, anyway? I didn't hear her any-where, just smelled the fresh coffee. I strapped on my shoul-der holster, threw on my suit and shoes, then walked out of the bedroom into a short hallway. I'd never been to her place before, here on what they called Pill Hill near a bunch of hospitals around Madison Street, but the apartment wasn't all that large and I soon found Miss Jenkins just two doors down the hall in the kitchen.

She was dressed in a red-and-black plaid bathrobe with matching slippers, and sat facing the doorway at a small, chrome-legged table set under a frilly curtained window. She was smoking a cigarette, something she hardly ever did. The smell of java came from the percolator sitting on the nearby stove. She looked gorgeous as ever, even with her hair slightly mussed, and seemed lost in thought, had a bit of a winsome look on her pretty face.

Half of me wanted to beat feet right out the door, but instead, I cheerfully said, "Morning, doll."

She glanced up, smiled, and then replied, a touch wariness to her tone, "How are you?"

"Fine," I said, stepping into the kitchen. I pointed at her pack of cigarettes. "Those things will stunt your growth, you know."

She didn't say anything, just tapped the ash off of her half-finished smoke.

"I had a terrific time last night," I told her, approaching the table.

"You did?" she asked softly.

"Oh, yeah. Too bad I don't remember much about it."

"What?"

"Oh, I remember us out dancing, well enough. What happened after that?"

"You don't remember?"

I stopped across from her at the edge of the table. "Can't say as I do. I did a lot of drinking. I must have blacked out."

Her face fell a bit. "Well, we both drank a lot, I guess."

"Sure did," I said, pulling out my smokes and lighting up. "I do recall my birthday dinner, though. Clear as a bell. Nicest present I've ever had. It's after that where it gets all hazy."

"We took a taxi here to my place," said Miss Jenkins. "We had too much to drink to drive. We played some music on my hi-fi and had a nightcap and—"

"You were nice enough to put me to bed," I told her. "Sorry for tying one on."

"That's O.K." She stubbed out her cigarette.

"But I'm sure I was a perfect gentleman, huh?"

"Yes," she said quietly. "You were."

"Good. Wouldn't do to—"

"No," she said, abruptly standing up. "To tell you the truth, I don't remember much of anything myself."

"You don't? Well, now, that's—"

"Excuse me," she said. "I think I may have left the water running in the bathroom."

"I don't hear anything."

She hurried out of the kitchen.

Chapter

12

THE FEDERAL COURTHOUSE WAS STILL
pretty new. Finished about 1940, it sat on Fifth Avenue just
a few blocks from the downtown waterfront

I parked, plugged a couple nickels in the meter, and went in
for my meeting with Judge Torrence. The courthouse hadn't
changed much, still had an almost palpable air of tension to
it once you got through the big, revolving main door. Never
could quite put my finger on what made it that way. My best
guess was that it housed a number of offices and places that
just naturally put people a little on edge—the federal courts,
the federal prosecutor's office, etc., etc.—most folks going in
and out of the building had business with one or another
of those branches of government, business that produced a
general anxiety that tinged the atmosphere like a tuning fork
or fingernail being scratched across a blackboard.

I felt more than a little of that myself as I made my way
back to the glass-fronted index listing the location of the
building's many offices. I kept thinking that the statute of
limitations must have run out on the bootlegging allegations
from my old booze route in downtown Seattle. They didn't
have enough to formally charge me, and let me walk. I was
sure I'd beaten that rap long ago. Only other thing I could

think of was koshing the G-man who'd butted into my first case back in '39. Couldn't be that: I'd blindsided him in an alley a couple days after he told me to lay off my own case. He never knew what hit him.

Damn. Had to be some good reason a federal judge wanted to see me. But what about, I just didn't know. All I knew, at the moment, was that I was low on smokes, and didn't want to run out if things got dicey. That, of course, was an illogical thought—I hadn't done anything wrong lately—but that was the effect that a summons to the Federal Courthouse could have on you.

I stopped by the small snack shop in the main foyer before catching the elevator to the federal courts on the second floor. There, I picked up two packs of cigarettes from the old blind man who ran the shop. He was the same joe who ran the place when I was here the last time, just after the war. A little more wrinkled, and a little more bald, I marveled again at how he knew where a particular brand of smokes was placed on his shelves. He just reached back, easy as you please, and fished two packs of Philip Morrises out of the dozen or so varieties that he stocked.

Not having enough coins, I handed him a dollar bill for the smokes. "Keep the change, Pops."

He smiled, then paused, running the fingers of one hand back and forth across the greenback. "You sure?" he asked. "This is a fiver."

I looked closely at the bill. Damned if he wasn't right. I'd given him a five dollar bill by mistake. How he knew it was beyond me.

"I don't meet many honest men in my line of work," I told him. "What the hell? I'm flush. Keep it anyway."

"Jeez, thanks, mister," he said as I left.

Having done my good deed for the day, I caught the elevator for my appointment with the judge.

His judicial chambers were dark and foreboding. The walls were paneled in a walnut-stained wood that seemed to be closing in on me no matter how spacious his chambers actually were. The furnishings were about as dark as the woodwork—deep brown, almost black, leather chairs sat across from his large desk, which was made from some kind of wood that was even a shade darker than the paneling. Even the glass-fronted bookcases that lined most of the walls were dismal and added to the oppressive feel of the judge's office, all the law books in them heavy with the weight of the nation's myriad laws. I always wondered why there were so damned many of them—especially since the basic ten had been more than good enough for old Moses.

Judge Torrence, himself, was somewhat imposing, dressed as he was in his long, shiny, black robe. He rose to his feet behind his desk when I came in. My first impression of him was that he stood ramrod straight, had a firm handshake, and was square jawed and handsome. My second impression was that he had very cold, blue eyes and a narrow, rather disingenuous smile. Somewhere in his mid-forties, he seemed all wound up and tense underneath that tight grin.

"You're prompt, Mr. Rossiter," he told me. "I like that. I often find promptness to be the measure of the man."

"What can I do for you, judge?"

"Direct, too," he said, arching an eyebrow. "Cut to the chase, straight to the point. Yes," he added, looking me up and down like he liked the cut of my jib. "You'll do quite nicely."

"Thanks. But if you don't mind me asking again: *what*, exactly, do you think I'm quite nicely cut out to do for you?"

He laughed. Had himself a real gut-buster. The huge guffaw was way out of proportion to my small bit of wit—was the type of laugh that usually waited for the slightest excuse to release a whole load of built up tension.

"Have a seat, Mr. Rossiter," he said, sitting back behind his desk. "Join me for a drink. I know you're a drinking man."

"How do you know that?" I asked, sitting down in the leather wingback across from his desk.

"I've had you checked out, of course."

"Of course." He was one up on me. I knew I should've checked him out, too, whether I had short notice for this appointment or not.

"I have a good Glenfiddich," he said, withdrawing a bottle of the cost-you-a-week's-pay hooch from the small liquor cabinet just to the right of his desk. He fished out two, cut-crystal glasses, as well, and set everything up on his green, felt desk pad. "A wonderfully heady single malt," he told me, uncapping the bottle. "I know you like Scotch."

"I usually go for blended," I said.

"Blended?" He said the word as if it was beneath him.

"Yeah. Cutty. Dewar's in a pinch."

"Well, I'm afraid I don't have any of *those*. You should really try the Glenfiddich, broaden your palate."

"O.K. Knock yourself out, judge." I gestured for him to pour me a snort. "Broaden my palate."

He handed me a glass of the heavy, peaty malt. I'd had it before. Didn't much like it. It was the kind of ritzy stuff, in my experience, that a lot of folks drank just to show off.

Not Judge Torrence, though. He really seemed to enjoy it—that is, if how fast he swilled down his first glass and quickly poured himself another belt was any measure of true enjoyment.

"Ah, that's better," he said, relaxing a bit for the first time. "How do you find your Scotch, Mr. Rossiter?"

"It is what it is." I took a polite sip.

"Indeed," he agreed, keeping his glass in his hand as he nursed his second drink. His gaze drifted over to the large, framed photograph that hung on the dark, paneled wall near my chair. The judge's eyes softened slightly as he stared at the photo: a headshot of none other than J. Edgar Hoover, the country's top G-Man. It was signed, also had some type of inscription written under J. Edgar's bold signature that I couldn't quite make out from where I was sitting.

"FBI Director sign that just for you?" I asked.

"Yes," the judge said, not taking his eyes off of the photo.

"How about that?" I walked over and perused the sentiment written at the bottom of J. Edgar's beefy mug:

Congratulations on your appointment to the federal bench. I know that you will continue the good fight. This agency shall never be further than a phone call away.

"How long ago did you get this?" I asked.

"Summer of '36," the judge told me as I returned to my seat.

"You were pretty young."

"Yes. Thirty-two. I was the youngest judge ever appointed to the federal bench."

"That's something. Must be good at what you do."

"I am."

"I am, too. So, what can I do for you? Way you've been staring at Mr. Hoover, looks like you'd like to take him up on his offer of a phone call."

"I wish I could."

"What's that supposed to mean?"

"To a great degree, my problem has to do with Mr. Hoover."

"How so?"

The judge leaned back in his chair, and sighed.

"Early this year, Mr. Rossiter, the FBI issued a directive to all levels of the federal government. Put simply, a campaign has begun to identify and dismiss any Communists and homosexuals from all levels of government service."

"How does that affect you?"

He smiled. "Let's just say that I am not a Communist."

"Oh," I said.

"Yes," he told me. "At first, I thought there wasn't much to worry about. It would all begin with a big show, then fizzle out. So many things the government starts, it never finishes, you know? But not in this case. It's just been getting worse and worse. A real witch-hunt. I didn't know what to do. Then, I saw your picture in the paper yesterday and—"

"Oh, hell . . ."

"—and I knew that I had to see you after I read the story."

"Look, judge, let's get one thing straight, here. I may be helping Donny and Martin out, but I'm not—"

"Whether you share our persuasion, or not, Mr. Rossiter, is your business. That's something each of us has to deal with individually. But, at the very least, I knew that I could trust you. After checking into your background and character, I was even more confident of that." He paused and leaned across the desk toward me, a little fear and hope all mixed together in his eyes. "I trust I'm not mistaken," he said quietly.

"Yeah, you can count on me," I said, getting up out of my chair even though I wasn't planning on going anywhere quite yet. "What we talk about is just between you and me and nobody else—just like all my clients."

"I knew it," he said. "I didn't doubt it for a minute." He took a deep breath, and knocked off the Scotch he'd been sipping in one big slug. "I can't tell you how good it is to have someone to confide in."

"So, start confiding," I said. "What you've told me is all fine and dandy, but I'm still in the dark as to what you think I can do for you. If you're trying to put me between you and the FBI, forget it. I don't butt heads with the feds without a damned good reason. Usually not even then."

"I'm being blackmailed."

"O.K., that's more up my alley," I told him. "Who's blackmailing you?"

"I don't know this time."

"*This time?*" I sat back down across from him. "You've been blackmailed before?"

"Yes."

"Same reason?"

"Yes."

"And you knew who did it the first time?"

"Yes."

"Who was it?"

"Trixie," he said, a tinge of sadness in his voice. "It was Trixie."

I felt like I'd just been slugged in the gut by the Brown Bomber.

"Trixie, huh? Same Trixie who worked at the Garden of Allah?"

"That's right," he said.

"You must have been plenty upset about the blackmail."

"I didn't kill her, if that's what you're thinking—though the thought did cross my mind on occasion."

"What did Trixie have on you, judge?"

"Photographs. A number of them. Some quite compromising. They were taken at last year's Bacchanalia at Royce Bennington's."

"Bennington, huh? Just how compromising were these photos?"

"I was wearing a toga and nothing else." He looked me straight in the eye. "In some, I wasn't even wearing the toga."

"I see."

"Trixie and I used to be lovers," he volunteered.

"That right? So, it was Trixie and you in these snaps?"

"Yes."

"In that case," I asked, "who was the shutterbug?"

"I don't know."

"Must have been some flashbulbs going off."

He was quiet a moment, sipped at his drink, then shook his head. "I was otherwise engaged, if you know what I mean. To tell you the truth, I remember very little about the whole evening."

"Try harder."

"It's just no use, I tell you. All I recall is a blur of drinking and dancing and smoking and waking up the next morning in one of the upstairs bedrooms with Trixie."

"That where the photos were taken?"

He looked insulted. "Well, of course. I'm not the type to cavort in public. Some do, but I find that very gauche."

"Indeed," I said. "Looks like you were set up, your Honor. Fair guess whoever took those snaps is the one who's blackmailing you now."

"Yes, I've thought of that."

"How long had Trixie been doing the number on you?"

"The blackmail, you mean?" he asked. "A few months. It all started right after we broke up."

"Jilted him, huh?"

"I had to," he told me. "This government witch-hunt going on, I couldn't take any chances. I've been a perfect homebody ever since. I've been going out only with my wife. Made a point to be seen with her in public more than ever before. Francine is quite a bit younger than me. She loves going out. She's always wanted children, too, and I'm happy to say that she's finally gotten her wish. She's pregnant for the first time."

"Well, congrats," I said. "Shouldn't be any feds looking sideways at you with a young, pregnant wife."

He gave me a sour look. "What's the harm? I've given Francine what she's always wanted, and I do have to protect myself."

"I take it your wife's not aware that you like men."

"Good God, of course not." He flipped open the large, gold cigarette case that sat on his desk, and withdrew a smoke from the fifty or so fags it contained. He offered me one, but I passed and fired up my own brand while he lit his with the big, round table-model lighter that matched the cigarette case.

"Was Trixie still blackmailing you when he was killed?" I asked.

"No," he said, sucking down his first drag like his life depended on it. "I'd made the last payment and gotten all the photos back just before she was murdered."

"You never make the *last* payment to most blackmailers. They usually come back to haunt you."

"I'm finding that out," he told me. "But I'd gotten every photo, and the negatives, as well."

"Easy enough to make copies. You can even do up fresh negatives from the copies if you want."

He sighed. "Two more photos arrived the day before yesterday."

"Was there a note with them?"

"No. They came to my chambers by courier—plain brown envelope with no return address. I got a phone call about them a little later."

"Man or a woman?"

"I couldn't tell. The voice was very low and muffled, like they had the mouthpiece covered with a handkerchief or something. The person demanded five thousand dollars."

"Couple year's wages for the average joe," I mused. "You got that kind of dough?"

"I'd give ten times that amount if this would only stop," he said. "Will you please help me, Mr. Rossiter? They said if I don't pay, they'll turn the photos over to the newspapers. I'd be ruined."

"Yeah, I'll see what I can do," I told him, finding the unexpected connection to Trixie and Royce Bennington plenty damned intriguing.

"Thank God."

"Where are you supposed to drop the money, judge?" I asked.

"At the Greyhound bus depot tonight," he told me. Then he filled me in on the details, reached into his desk and pulled out a check that was already made out to me. "Here," he said, handing it over. The check was made out for four bills. "I trust that's sufficient, Mr. Rossiter."

"It's sufficient." I folded it and put it in my pocket.

"I'll double that amount when you're successful," he told me. "Now," he said, glancing at his wristwatch, "I'm a busy man and must get back to work. As, I'm sure, *you* must as well," he added, pointedly.

I took the hint. I left Judge Torrence's chambers not only feeling highly relieved, but actually damned glad I'd been summoned to meet him. The four bills in my pocket felt a whole lot better than the fines that joes like him usually meted out. Felt so good, in fact, that I took myself straight to the nearest bar, which happened to be a dive called Bernie's, a couple blocks down on the edge of skid road. There, no Cutty or Dewars in the joint, I celebrated my good fortune with a watered-down shot that the barkeep called his best Scotch.

I was working on my third shot, when my gut started to ache. The barkeep said it wasn't his rotgut that had caused it and, being in increasingly bad shape to argue with him, I blew the joint back to my car. I was barely behind the wheel when the first wave of nausea hit me. It wasn't too bad, but after driving a few blocks, the second wave was worse. Couple blocks later, I almost upchucked.

I would've normally just swilled some Pepto and toughed it out. But I got to thinking that I might have gotten some tainted moonshine. A lot of joints—especially the low-down, sleazy ones like I'd just been in—still bought homemade when they could find it, which was pretty often. Some of that shit could make you go blind or worse. Way I was feeling, I wasn't taking any chances. I managed to steer the Roadmaster the half-mile to Seattle General and paid a call to their emergency services.

Luckily, they weren't very busy that time of the morning. Still, it took them the better part of an hour to bring me the results of their blood-drawing, poking, prodding, and temperature-taking for no good reason.

"Mr. Rossiter," said the peach-fuzz resident as he came into the examining room where I'd been hovering over my stainless-steel barf-pan, wearing only my underwear, for what seemed an eternity. "How do you feel?"

"Stupid question," I told him. He was taken aback, didn't know quite what to say. "Sorry, doc," I said. "Guess I'm better—haven't made a deposit in my pan yet."

"You're lucky," he said, flipping through the pages in the clipboard he held.

"Oh, yeah?"

"Yes. You didn't drink any wood alcohol or such, but the state your liver's in, you may as well have."

"What?" I turned to face him directly—kept my pan in front of me just in case. "What's wrong with my liver?"

"Everything," he said, pushing his drooping spectacles back up on the bridge of his small and narrow nose. "Well, not quite," he laughed. I wasn't amused. "Sorry," he said. "Look, your liver enzymes are all out of whack. They're extremely elevated. How much do you drink on a daily basis?"

"Never keep track."

"I advise you to start keeping track, Mr. Rossiter. As in limiting your alcoholic intake to one or two drinks per week at most."

"Per week? You've got to be kidding."

"Abstinence would be best," he droned on. "Let me look in your eyes again, will you?"

"Why the eyes?" I asked, as he came at me with his tiny instrument with its blinding light. "What do they have to do with my liver?"

"Nothing," he said, peering into each one of them. "Except

for the slight jaundice in them." Finished, he slipped the instrument back into his top pocket. "You used to be a boxer, you said," he told me.

"Yeah, that's right."

"Good thing you stopped."

"I can take a punch with the best of them."

"That's just the point," he said, with an irritating, patronizing tone. "I won't bore you with the specifics, but you've taken too many blows to the head over the years." He paused, looked at his papers again. "And what is it you do for a living, now?"

"I'm a private detective."

"Oh, yes, that's right. Do you ever get hit in the head in your line of work?"

"Sometimes the other guy gets lucky."

He closed his clipboard. "I strongly advise you to look for another type of job."

"I'm supposed to lay off the sauce and take up driving a trolley, too, huh?"

He laughed. "Or anything else you're qualified for."

"What a crock!" I tossed the barf-pan on the examining table. "I'm outta here."

"Mr. Rossiter," he said, holding a hand up. "Wait, you don't—"

"Better stay out of my way," I told him, grabbing my trousers, "or you'll end up needing your own services."

I got out of there in short order. When they sent me the bill, I'd tear it up or send it right back to them. I had enough to worry about without overpriced, bad advice.

Miss Jenkins was out when I got back to the office, which was just as well—I wanted some private time at my desk, alone with my bottle, no small talk, no messages, and no interruptions. I hated quacks. What did they know, anyway? I'd been drinking and fighting all my life, that was just the way of things. My stomach had felt better almost as soon as I'd gotten out of the hospital. I'd had a little touch of the stomach flu or bad indigestion, that's all.

I settled in behind my desk and poured myself a stiff shot of Cutty. It hit the spot. Frigging overpaid quacks. What's to worry? I'd never been beaten in the ring, and all the Japs in the Pacific hadn't been able to kill me. Drinking a little Scotch wasn't going to do anything except take some of the edge off.

I suddenly felt nauseas again. I scrambled to the head.

After hugging the toilet bowl for a good ten minutes, it passed. I took the Pepto out of my medicine cabinet and drank straight from the bottle.

I felt much improved as I returned to my desk where I capped my fifth of Cutty Sark and put it back in my desk drawer. I checked the time, wondered where the hell Miss Jenkins was—she was usually in by now. That's when I heard the main entry door to the outer office open and close. Figuring she'd finally blown in, I was really surprised when the door to my inner office flew open. A tall man, early fifties, wearing a sour expression and a camel-hair overcoat barged in.

"Are you Jake Rossiter?" he asked, heading my way in a hurry.

I got to my feet. "Who the hell are you?"

"Abe Horowitz," he told me. Instead of a handshake, he finished the introduction by plunking his heavy, satchel-style briefcase directly down on top of my desk.

"Well, it's good to meet you at last, Mr. Horowitz," I said, a small wave of nausea returning. "My operative, Heine, is just in the process of preparing a report for you on—"

"These are for you," he cut me off, withdrawing a large, manila envelope from his briefcase, which he tossed in front of me.

"What's this?"

"Open it."

The envelope contained about a dozen, 8×10, glossy, black & white photos. Every one of them showed Heine and Lorna Horowitz together. They were kissing in some; out drinking and dancing in others; one showed them making out in the front seat of Heine's Ford; and a couple had actually caught them in bed together—the two explicit pics had been taken through the parted Venetian blinds of an outside window, and were rather underexposed, but you could still make out the lovebirds and their disrobed hanky-panky just dandy.

"I hired your agency to get the goods on my cheating wife," intoned Horowitz. "Not *sleep* with the little tramp!"

"Where'd you get these?"

"I suspected something was off, so I hired another private detective to follow your man," he told me. "Needless to say, you won't be getting a thin dime from me. I may just sue you for all you're worth."

"Hold on," I said. "I can explain—"

"There's nothing to explain," said Horowitz. "Goodbye!" With that, he tramped out of the office, and slammed the door.

Chapter

13

FRIGGING HEINE. I WANTED TO JUST REAM him. It wasn't bad enough that he'd missed my birthday and told me to fuck myself. Now he'd gone and cost us the dough from Horowitz that I'd been counting on.

I decided to blow off some steam and go find Dennis Diamond. I had cash in hand from Rollo Mudd for this case at least. I figured I'd start at Club Rialto and work out from there.

As I headed downtown, I noticed an indigo sedan tailing me. Whoever was driving didn't know much about pulling a tail. The sedan, a late model Pontiac, followed me too close, and matched my every move.

The light ahead turned yellow as I hit the intersection of First & Pike. I gunned the Roadmaster through it and watched my rear-view. The Pontiac ran the red behind me in order to keep up. Then I sped up even more, turned right at the next corner, but slowed way down so that the tail would be right on me as he came out of the corner in my slipstream.

Tires squealing through the turn, the Pontiac suddenly found itself right on my butt. I caught my first good glimpse of the driver and made him immediately: none other than big Sammy, Rollo Mudd's goon, his eyes as wide as his beef-cake mug at finding himself right on top of me.

Why the follow, I didn't know. But I'd soon find out.

I hit the brakes hard. So did Sammy, but not fast enough to keep from rear-ending me. As crashes go, it wasn't much, but it did cause Sammy to bite through the stogie that was in his mouth. Bailing out, I reached his driver's door while he was still madly fishing around for the smoldering cigar somewhere in his lap.

As I pulled his door open, he stammered—"What the fuck? What the fuck?"—alternating the question between my sudden appearance and the lost stogie that was threatening to torch his gonads.

"You should learn to pull a better tail," I told him.

"What?"

"You were following me too close."

"You wise-ass, I'll...Oww, sonofabitch!" he yelled, burning a few fingers as he finally located the stogie.

"Ought to learn to drive better, too, Sammy."

"What?" he asked, stuffing the stogie into the ashtray, and brushing at his pants. "What the hell are you talking about?"

"Like I said, you were following too close. Hand over your insurance info; I'll be filing a claim."

To that, he didn't really say anything—just made guttural sounds and started to come out of the car at me. I impeded his progress by shutting the door on his left leg, and leaned most of my weight against it while he made another series of even more guttural sounds.

"Why were you following me?" I asked him, as more than a few passers by stopped to gawk.

"Fuck you!" He followed up the epithet with some moans and groans.

I leaned a little harder against the door and repeated my question. "Why were you following me? This your idea or Rollo Mudd's?"

He struggled a mite more, then wisely stopped. "Mine," he said, through gritted teeth.

"Now we're getting somewhere." I took a bit of the pressure off the door. "Why?"

"I don't trust you, dammit!"

"Tell me something I don't know."

"Hey, mac!" yelled a young joe from the other side of the street. Dressed in paint-splattered, white coveralls and a matching painter's cap, he'd evidently come from the nearby Pike Place Market, and carried an open butcher-paper parcel filled with a string of frankfurters that he was munching on. "You O.K. over there?"

"Sure," I said. "We're just passing the time of day."

"I saw it happen," hollered the young painter. "You got your bumpers locked. That guy giving you trouble? You need a witness?"

"How about it?" I asked Sammy. "You still giving me trouble?"

He grimaced, shoved against the door again, but still couldn't free his leg. "You went to the Federal Courthouse," he told me. "What business you got with the feds?"

"That's for me to know, and you to find out."

"I'm tellin' Mr. Mudd. He ain't gonna like it."

"He isn't going to like you with your leg in a cast, either, you dumb mook."

I was just about to prepare the limb for the plaster, when a traffic cop roared up in front of me and hopped off his motorcycle. Tall and skinny as Ichabod Crane, his ticket-book in hand, he asked, "Trouble, here?"

"Not at all, officer," I said. "We were just exchanging insurance information." I turned and pulled the door open for Sammy. "Isn't that right, Mr. Sammy?"

He glared at me—slowly got out of the Pontiac, mightily favoring his leg and rubbing at its shinbone. "Yeah," he mumbled. "Yeah."

"You hurt in the accident, mister?" asked the cop, his extra-large Adam's apple working like a pile driver as he spoke.

"Nah," said Sammy. "It's nothin'."

"I saw it all," ventured the young painter, hurrying up to us from across the street. Taking half a frankfurter in one big bite, he said, "That guy in the Pontiac, he just tore around the corner and rear-ended this guy in the Buick."

"That so," said the cop, giving Sammy a stern glance.

"Yes, unfortunately," I volunteered. "Bumpers bent and locked, and me late for an important appointment." I smiled. "But not to worry: Mr. Sammy, here, just kindly offered to pay me in cash for the damages. Doesn't want to bother his insurance company, if you know what I mean, officer."

"What?" said Sammy.

"Looked like that big joe was trying to fight with this guy, officer," said the painter.

"That so?" repeated the cop, giving Sammy the evil eye.

"No, no," Sammy said. "I just, uh, caught my leg getting out. That's right, I was gonna pay him, that's right."

The cop thought a moment, then shrugged. "No skin off my nose. That's fine by me if that's what you want to do," he told me.

"Yes, it'd save a lot of trouble," I said. I took a quick gander at the bumpers, figured it was no more than twenty-five dollars in damage, and said, "A hundred bucks ought to cover it."

"A C-note!" Sammy exclaimed.

"I'll still have to give you a ticket, buddy," the cop told him.

"Judas Priest."

"Be quick about it, my good man," I told him, sticking out a palm for the dough. "I really must be hurrying along. Oh, also, you're big and strong, perhaps you could help me unlock the bumpers while you're at it."

"Hurry it up," said the traffic cop, starting to write Sammy's license plate number in his ticket book. "I haven't got all day."

Sammy grudgingly took out his wallet and handed over the cash—almost all the moola in his billfold, I happily noted. Then he and I stepped between the cars. I didn't even get a chance to help. With one mighty push, he shoved the Road-master's rear end down and the bumper popped free of the Pontiac's. I had the tiniest of dents by my license plate. The Pontiac's fender, however, was bashed in real good under the bumper where it had ridden up on my car. I also noticed more than a little fluid leaking from its radiator.

"I'll get ya for this, Rossiter," he hissed at me.

"Thank you, my good man," I told him, with a flourish of my fedora. "These things happen to the best of us. No hard feelings."

I climbed into the Roadmaster, nodded pleasantly to the cop and the painter, then drove off, feeling quite pleased with everything except for what Sammy was going to tell Rollo Mudd about my visit to the Federal Courthouse.

Chapter

14

THE STREETS WERE PRETTY PACKED, AND I had to park about a block up from the club. Plugging a few nickels into the meter, I prepared to go looking for Dennis Diamond, when *he* found me.

"Rossiter," said a deep voice, close behind me.

I spun around, faced a smiling man only about three feet away from me. He was roughly my age and height, had a muscular, athletic build, and wore a black & white houndstooth sports coat with a dark shirt and yellow tie. A large, diamond stickpin secured his tie; his gold cuff links were studded with big diamonds; he wore three diamond rings—two huge ones on the middle finger of each hand, and another, with a diamond about the size of my Buick, on the pinky-finger of his right hand.

"Dennis Diamond," he introduced himself, smiling even broader as he extended a hand for me to shake.

"I figured." I shook with him, but briefly.

He kept the happy face, then pulled a switchblade out of nowhere and flipped it open. Much to my relief, he used it nonchalantly to clean under a couple of his manicured fingernails as he continued the conversation.

"I've been hearing things about you. Good things. Interesting things," he said, deftly cleaning each nail with quick flicks of the six-inch blade. "I'd like to buy you a nice lunch."

"I tend to lose my appetite around pig-stickers," I told him.

He laughed. "Sorry. Force of habit. I always like to look my best." He folded the knife and put it back in his pocket.

"You been tailing me, like your boy, Sammy?" I asked.

"He's not my boy," said Diamond, losing the smile. "He's Rollo's stooge. No finesse. By the way, how *was* Judge Torrence?"

"How do you know—"

"I get around." His smile returned. "So, how about that lunch? I know a swell spot."

"I bet you do," I said, edgy and watching his every move.

"Don't be nervous. It's just lunch."

"Why?"

"Why not? We'll have some de-*luxe* grub and shoot the breeze." He didn't wait for me to agree, just turned toward the street and gave a high sign with his right hand. On command, a sleek, black Lincoln shot out of a parking place close down the way, and motored to the curb in front of us. I wouldn't have liked the look of the hood at the wheel most any time—a bulked up heavyweight, with arms as big around as my legs, wearing a slouch hat and an expression like Jersey Joe Walcott just before a fight—but right now, offering to give me a ride, I liked his looks even less.

"I'll drive," I told Diamond. "We'll take my wheels."

Diamond shrugged, strolled over to the Lincoln, and told his man, "Park it. Wait. I'll be back."

As the Lincoln slid into a spot a few cars up, we got into my Roadmaster. "Where to?" I asked.

"Pampas Grill," he said. "Up on Fourth & Pine. Folks there will treat us right."

He leaned back into the mohair as I pulled out into traffic, and lit up a long, black cheroot. He slowly puffed at it, inhaling the strong-ass smoke, I noted, and didn't say another word on the short drive uptown to the Pampas Grill. Neither did I. I just kept one eye out for any sudden movements on his part, and the other on the road, figuring he'd volunteer the reason for our impromptu lunch in good order.

I hadn't been to the Pampas but twice. Both times before they'd had the big fire last year. That it had been arson, was no question. But the insurance coughed up because the owner had an airtight alibi, and the place had been a going concern, had no financial troubles whatsoever. Nobody, not the arson squad nor the insurance investigators, could ever find a single motive as to why the owner would've torched his own establishment. The joint was rebuilt even bigger and nicer than before, and started doing record business. Which was good, considering the roughly four months revenues they'd lost.

It always smacked of a strong-arm job to me. Typical shake-down for protection.

My long-held suspicions were confirmed the instant Diamond and I walked in for lunch.

"*Mr. Diamond*," said the maître d', acting like the Pope himself had just blown in. He came out from behind his station and hurried up toward us past the dozen or so folks standing in line to be seated. "I wish I'd known you were coming."

"You *never* know when I'm coming," Diamond told him.

The dark-suited maître d' looked startled. He recovered in a flash; forced a grin and a chuckle. "Very true. Very true, indeed, Mr. Diamond. Come this way, your usual table is waiting, of course. I never seat anyone there except you."

"Of course," said Diamond, throwing me a wink.

As we followed the guy, a middle-aged, business type at the head of the line said, "Hey, I think I was next."

Hardly pausing, the maître d' answered, "And so shall you be, sir. This gentleman has a standing reservation."

"You don't take reservations for lunch."

The man added something else, but we were long gone, being seated at a large, wrought iron table under a tall, stained glass window depicting an Argentinean gaucho throwing a bolo. The place was packed, nary an empty seat in the house, busboys and waiters, all dressed like gauchos, hurried to and fro, their black-booted heels clicking up a clatter against the brittle, red tile floor. Even so, at the snap of the maître d's fingers, a busboy immediately appeared to fill our water goblets. Our waiter, young, mustachioed and swarthy, his gaucho hat worn at a jaunty angle, was right behind him.

"Hello, gentlemen," he said, taking his order book out of his bright, multi-colored vest.

"Hi, yourself, Victor," said Diamond, with a warm smile. "How's biz?"

"Never better," said the waiter, very cheerful. "Will you start with the usual, Mr. Diamond?"

"Yeah, the usual," he said. "Make it two."

"What's the usual?" I asked.

"Hot tea," the waiter told me. "A nice Darjeeling."

"Tea, huh?" I said. "O.K. Fine by me."

"And the meal?" the waiter asked. "Will that be the usual, as well?"

"*Si. Gracias,*" said Diamond, rolling the *r* like a native. "*Dos.*"

I didn't think he'd take me out to a Latin spot for tea and crumpets and little cucumber sandwiches, but, at the risk of repeating myself, I asked, "What's the usual?"

"*The Gaucho Special,*" Diamond told me.

"Tenderloins of beef skewered on a sword," the waiter explained. "Prime cuts, very rare, flambéed at the table."

"They do it with a real flourish," said Diamond. "Same with the vegetables. You'll like it." He glanced back at the waiter. "A pitcher of sangria with the meal, like always, Victor. And I'll take my regular salad."

"Salad for you, sir?" the waiter asked me. When I nodded yes, he added, "Your choice of dressing?"

"Blue cheese."

"Very well," he said. "I'll be right back with your tea, Mr. Diamond."

No sooner had our waiter left, than two men hurried out through the double-doors that I assumed led into the kitchen. The first, dressed all in black, with high boots, a gaucho hat with silver conchos, and a bright red kerchief around his neck, carried a large guitar, and took a seat on the high stool set in the center of the dining area. He began playing some type of classical music on guitar, as the other man beat feet up to our table. About fifty, and bald as a cue ball, he wore an impeccably tailored, gray, double-breasted suit, with a pink carnation boutonnière. When he arrived in front of us, I noted great beads of sweat dripping from his hairless pate down across his forehead.

"Needn't hurry on my account, Adolph," Diamond told him. "You'll get that asthma kicking up again."

"Señor Diamond," Adolph said, a bit out of breath. "I didn't see you last week."

"That's because I wasn't here."

"Ah," said Adolph, looking relieved, but casting furtive, nervous glances my direction. "I thought I missed you."

"I missed you, too." Diamond laughed at his own, small joke. "Meet my associate, Jake Rossiter."

"Glad to meet you," said Adolph, even though he looked like he wasn't.

Diamond put his right hand out, rubbed his fingers together. "I take it you've got something for me."

Adolph pulled two envelopes from his inside coat pocket and filled Diamond's hand with them.

"*Gracias.*"

"*Da nada.*"

"Very generous is old Adolph," Diamond told me.

"And, of course, lunch is on the house," said Adolph.

"Of course," said Diamond.

"Well, I must be getting back to my guests," he said, then hurried away.

"One of the nicest restauranteurs I know," Diamond told me.

"I see," I said, wondering just how much payoff was in each of the envelopes. "Why don't we get down to it, Diamond? I doubt you invited me out just to eat."

He threw me a little toast with his teacup. "Hey, any joe trying to help find my main squeeze is my pal—deserves a de-*luxe* meal. You get a line on her, yet, by any chance?"

"You should know if you've been following me."

"I treat my pals right," he told me. "You find Dolores, there's a two-bill bonus in it for you. Plus," he continued, his face darkening. "You find the bastard who murdered Trixie, and hand 'em over to me, there's even more dough for you. Lots more."

"What was Trixie to you, Diamond?"

"That's my business."

"Where were you when he was killed?"

He suddenly tensed. Went all tight-jawed and balled both hands into fists. "Any other joe, I'd slap silly for a remark like that."

"That any way to treat a pal?" I asked.

He stared holes through me, his eyes like ice picks. Finally, he relaxed, saying, "Yeah, well, you're just trying to do your job, right?"

"So, where were you?"

"I was out looking for Dolores when Trixie bought the farm." He withdrew one of his cheroots. "I was out lots of places."

"Why'd she leave you?"

"Who? Dolores?" He lit his cigar, then leaned back in his chair and spoke very softly, almost wistfully, "Dames. Who can figure 'em? You try to give them everything, but they just shit on you."

"Trixie shit on you, too?"

"Nah. Never. She was only trying to get a leg up in the world. Finally was, too, winning that contest at the club and all."

I fired up a smoke of my own. "Why are you so concerned about who killed Trixie? What I understand, Trixie didn't like you. Not one little bit."

"She liked me fine," he said, fiddling with his pinky ring. "Just got hacked off one time when I was fooling around too much."

"You fool around often with Trixie?"

He abruptly leaned toward me. "What d'ya mean by that?"

"You know what I mean."

"You *are* gonna get cuffed you keep talking like that," he hissed.

I didn't budge an inch—just returned his glare, ready for anything he might throw.

At length, Diamond shook his head and gave out a sarcastic laugh. "Shit," he said, settling back into his chair and folding his arms. "C'mon, gimme a break, Rossiter. I went for Trixie's singing, that's all. She had a swell voice—real style. She could really send you."

"That so?"

"Yeah. You never heard her sing. Your loss."

I accepted his answer for the moment, as our salads arrived—mine with blue cheese dressing, his with a curious mix of blue on one side of the lettuce and what looked like French dressing on the other side.

Laying his cheroot, still smoking, into the ashtray, Diamond stuck a fork into his salad and said, "If I were you, I'd look into the other female impersonators for this rap. They had the most to lose."

"How's that?"

"The contest," he said, popping a cherry tomato into his mouth and biting down ever so slowly on it. He grinned when it burst. "I just love it when they squish in your mouth like that," he told me, wiping a bit of tomato juice off his lip. "Anyway, Trixie won the amateur contest and got the contract, right? It's simple: one of the other performers usually gets bumped when a major new talent comes along."

"Got anybody in particular in mind?"

"Wish I did; I'd be taking care of them myself." He paused. "How's your salad?"

"Good dressing."

"The Pampas makes it themselves. They get the blue cheese from one of the food distributors that old Rollo's got his hooks into. Imported all the way from Denmark. Only top rate."

"Food wholesalers too, huh? You and Rollo have your fingers in a lot of pies."

"We've got a hell of a lot of fingers, too," he said, then smirked at his bit of wit. "Tell ya, Rossiter," he went on, between bites of his lettuce. "I'd also check out the losers of that female impersonator contest. They get some awful sore losers now and then from what I understand."

"I might just do that," I told him. "Why so helpful?"

"Like I said, I try to take care of my pals." He stabbed the last salad out of his bowl, then added, "A joe named Adrian came in a close second to Trixie in that contest. She was so good that they wanted to try her out—hired her for a short gig. Fair bet Adrian will get Trixie's long-term contract now that she's out of the way. I was you, I'd take a hard look at this Adrian."

"You talk to Adrian, yet, Diamond?"

"Sure," he said. "Adrian claimed she was nowhere near the club when Trixie got bumped off. I didn't go easy on her, either, but she stuck to that story. Even so, I've got my doubts."

"You've been a busy boy, haven't you?" I pulled out my pocket notebook, had more than a few reservations about Diamond steering me along, but figured I should get what info I could, nevertheless. "Got a last name for this Adrian? Address to go along with it?"

"She just goes by the single name: Adrian," he told me. "Lives up on Capitol Hill. About a mile north of Trixie's old place. It's the Belmont Arms, corner of Belmont East and Harvard. Studio in the basement: number 2B."

I wrote it down just as the waiter arrived with our main course: small tenderloins of beef skewered onto two, short, flaming swords exactly as advertised. Specialty of the house or not, it made quite a stir in the restaurant as the waiter carried the burning swords over to our table, some of the other diners oohing and ahhing as he went by.

"Is this sharp or what?" said Diamond, smiling broadly, as the waiter's assistant placed a large, long platter on the table between us. The waiter deftly placed both swords onto the platter, the flames dying out almost immediately. Another helper showed up right on cue and laid plates of asparagus and baked potatoes in front of us.

"Is there anything else I can get you?" our waiter asked.

"This is fine," Diamond told him. "Couldn't be better."

"*Bon appetit*," said the waiter, then left with his crew.

"Dig in," said Diamond, taking one of the swords and pulling the meat off of it with his fork. "Get it while it's hot."

I followed suit. The beef was so damned tender and exquisite that we didn't say another word for a while. Just savored and enjoyed each buttery bite.

About halfway through the meal, Diamond paused and said, "This is what Dolores and I always had when we came here. It was her favorite."

"I imagine."

"Yeah," he said. "Yeah," he repeated, very softly. Then he lowered his head, dropped his knife and fork with a clatter, and started crying. Sobbed and cried like some little kid.

I usually had a quick comeback for most anything. But I

didn't really know what to do in this case. Here I was, sitting in a ritzy restaurant with a tough hood who was suddenly acting like he'd just lost his Mom. He wasn't really loud or hysterical about it, but did start to attract the attention of the other patrons seated nearby.

"Get a grip, Diamond," I said, at length.

"She's all I think about," he blubbered. "Dolores is everything…" He shook his head, then looked me right in the eye, both of his orbs bloodshot and running, a little snot starting to drip down his nose. "Sorry…sometimes I just can't handle it."

I gave him the big linen napkin off my lap. "Here. Clean yourself up. I'll find her for you, O.K.?"

"You promise?"

"I promise."

"Yeah?"

"Yeah."

Chapter

15

I HEADED FOR HEINE'S HOME AWAY FROM home, the pool hall at Ben Paris. Best pal or not, I felt like busting him in the chops—couldn't believe I'd ever feel this way about the guy who helped get me through the war. He'd saved my butt at least as many times as I'd saved his. Maybe more. We'd been together ever since we ran away from the orphanage at age fourteen. Good times and bad, we'd backed each other up from our days riding the rails and boxing smokers, to a stint as rumrunners, then finally starting out in the private eye business just before the war. Hell, we were more like brothers than friends.

That said, I decided not to slug him after all. If a brother can't tell you to go fuck yourself, who can? Plus, this was the first time I'd ever known Heine to be in love. He was just topsy-turvy, that's all—head over heels and out of his right mind. When he heard the news about Lorna's hubby, he'd come around. Besides, I needed him for a job. Namely, the stake-out on Judge Torrence's money-drop at the Greyhound bus station. Thought I'd see if I could get him back on track. I had to get somebody in place for that duty, anyway, as I'd be busy with other things. He could work his way back into my good graces, we'd solve the problem for the judge and make enough dough to make up for what he lost us over Lorna, and I could concentrate on my main case: solving Trixie's murder. To boot, if I still felt like slugging him, I could always slug him later.

I found Heine at a table in back of the nearly empty pool hall. The only other occupants were Stan, the daytime attendant, and two players wrapping up a game by the hall's entrance. As I entered, the older of the two, dressed slick and dapper, sunk the eight ball and stuck a palm out for some green. The younger man shook his head and obliged; filled the joe's hand with a double-sawbuck, then said, "That's it for me, bud."

"C'mon kid," the older man told him. "Give ya a chance to make it up. Double or nothing on the next game."

"Joe at that back table already gave me that chance," the kid told him, gesturing in Heine's direction. "I went double with that shark, then lost with you. Now I got nothing. I'm tapped. See ya."

"How about you, mister?" the hustler asked me as the kid left. "Fancy a game?"

"Got other business," I told him, then strode back toward Heine.

"Fucking economy," the guy grumbled as I walked past him. "Too many joes working. This place used to be packed right after the war."

Heine saw me coming. Didn't say anything. Just broke a new rack of balls as I approached.

"You're looking sharp," I said, referring to his crisply pressed slacks and brilliant white shirt, worn open at the neck under his silk sports coat. "New threads?"

"Yeah. Expensive, too." He eyed me for a second. "You pissed?"

"A little," I told him. "But I need you for a gig."

He didn't respond—ran three balls off the table, then chaulked his cue. "You ain't here about me and Lorna?"

"Not necessarily."

"Yeah, well, good. Don't get into it. Sorry I told you to get screwed, but I ain't taking any grief about her."

I lit a smoke. "Where is she, by the way? Thought I'd find you two together."

"Would've been," Heine said. "I was supposed to be taking her out this afternoon, but something came up. Said she'd get hold of me late tonight; we'd go out then."

"How late?"

"After nine or ten o'clock, she said. Why?"

"The job I want you to pull. You'll be done in plenty of time."

"O.K.," he said. "Long as I'm finished up by nine."

"Got a good idea what came up with Lorna if you want to hear it."

He frowned; tossed his cue on the table. "That's what you really came for, ain't it? Why are you pussy-footing around, Jake? Ain't like you."

"Just trying to get along with you, gyreen."

"O.K. What? Spit it out."

"Old man Horowitz is onto you two."

"That so?"

"He came by the office today and read me the riot act. He's got photos of you and his wife together."

"How the hell did he get those?"

"Got suspicious and hired himself another private dick. Private dick who did his job, I might add."

Heine was quiet a moment, then fired up one of his Luckys. "O.K., so maybe I deserved that jab," he told me. "But fuck it. This is good."

"It's good?"

"Yeah." He smiled. "Means me and Lorna can get married."

"Have you gone off your nut? What makes you think—"

"She loves me, I love her. Her husband will want a divorce now, which is what she's been waiting for."

"Heine, she's just been—"

"She don't care about money," he rambled on, getting all starry-eyed. "Told me so a million times. She just wanted her fair share."

"Heine—"

"I told her not to sweat it—I made plenty for the both of us—but she said she was only concerned about getting enough to set me up in my own business. 'Course, I'd never leave you, Jake, but, you know, ain't that swell, always thinking about me and not herself? Lorna's just one hell of a dame."

"Heine, compadre, I—"

"You'll come to our wedding won't ya?" he asked, walking around the table like he was on Cloud 9. "You and Miss Jenkins and everybody, right?"

If a man ever needed to be slugged, it was right then. Only I couldn't do it. He was just too damned happy, poor bastard.

"Sure, we'll all be at your wedding," I told him.

"That's great!" He wrapped me up in a bear hug—which was a real bear hug, big and stocky as he was.

Finally letting go of me, he said, "Damn, Jake, I really am sorry for getting all pissed at you. We're still pards, right?"

"Roger."

"Yeah, I knew a little thing like this wasn't gonna get between us." He flashed me his pearly whites. "I'll make it up to ya on that gig tonight. Do it gratis, even. What is it, anyway?"

I tipped my hat back on my head, thought about saying something else about his situation, then thought better of it. He was in for a fall and would have to take it for himself. Nothing I could say or do would be able to cushion his landing.

"Money drop on a blackmail," I said at length.

"Who's getting squeezed?" Heine asked.

"Federal judge."

"No shit? That's big-time."

"Yeah. But I think it's an amateur play."

"How so?"

"Drop's in a locker at the Greyhound bus station. Plenty of cover—easy stake-out."

"Who's delivering the money?"

"Judge himself. Five P.M."

"Copacetic. Should be a piece of cake," he said, sounding like the Heine of old.

"You nab the extortionist, you bring 'em to the office and sit on 'em," I told him. "I'll be back there by seven at the latest. No cops until we have a chance to talk to the judge."

"What if nobody shows?"

"The judge is supposed to leave the locker key on top of the phone booth in back by the men's lavatory. Blackmailer doesn't show, you pick up the key and the dough and bring it along to the office. I'll take from there if need be."

"You got it," said Heine, extending a hand. "But I'm bailing in time to meet Lorna no matter what. Understand?"

I shook with him—grip like a frigging bear trap and

a temperament to match—best damned man I ever knew. "Yeah, I understand."

"Glad we got this settled, jarhead," he told me with a big smile.

"Same-same," I said.

"Well, I'm gonna head out," he said, grabbing his fedora off one of the oak chairs lining the wall. "I'll be at the bus station a little early. Between now and then, I've got some phone calls to make."

"To who?" I asked, as we walked out together.

"Oh, a couple florists, some jewelers, few other places," he told me, fairly beaming. "Gotta go first rate for Lorna, you know. Might be a little early, but I'm gonna do this wedding better than right."

Chapter

16

I HAD A FEMALE IMPERSONATOR TO GRILL. Namely, this Adrian that Dennis Diamond had clued me to. The runner-up in that female impersonator contest would have had a decent motive for bumping off Trixie if they had a mind to. I felt like a dolt for not having thought of it sooner.

Before I did that, however, I stepped into the phone booth by Ben Paris's shoeshine stand and plugged in a nickel for the office. Four rings and it switched over to the answering service. Betty's southern drawl told me there were no messages, not from Miss Jenkins or anybody else. To keep Miss Jenkins up to speed, I left a message for her about what had happened with Abe Horowitz and how that whole damned case had now gone south. Then I left her another about Judge Torrence being blackmailed and told her that I had Heine staking out the money drop tonight in hopes of nabbing the blackmailer.

Finished, I checked my Bulova: it was pushing 4:00.

At 4:20, I rang the door buzzer at the Garden of Allah.

The red-haired organist let me into the club. "Donny in?" I asked him.

"No," he said.

"Where is he?"

"How would I know?" he said, a little snippy. "He never tells me anything—I'm just the organ player." He shook his head and sighed. "Look, sorry—things have been all fouled up around here ever since the murder. Donny was here a few minutes ago, then he took off. I imagine he's out trying to find Martin again."

"Adrian's really who I want to see," I said. "Is he here? I'd like to have a word with him."

"Adrian won't be on 'til five." Somebody rang the door-buzzer. "She's our opening act," he said, peering out the curtains, then letting two, young soldiers in, both wearing their dress uniforms. "Get yourself a drink in the bar," he told me, as the soldiers headed for one of the still sparsely populated tables. "I'll let her know you're here—see if she's got time to talk to you."

"Tell him to make time," I said. Then I went over and pulled up a high-backed chair at the long bar off to the right. A quick belt sounded good, anyway. If Adrian didn't come out to meet me by the time I finished it, I'd go backstage and meet him.

Two sips into my Scotch, my stomach was still feeling fine. As was my supposedly ailing liver. Fucking quacks, what'd they know?

A crew cut, blonde joe, wearing a blue silk bathrobe, slid into the chair beside me.

"I hear you were asking for me," he said.

Hell's bells, I thought, this was the same joe I'd seen getting cinched into his corset the night Trixie bought the farm.

"I knew you'd come back," he told me, all smiles. "Oh,

and you bought me a drink, too!" he exclaimed, grabbing my shot glass from the counter and knocking it back. "How sweet."

"You're Adrian, huh?"

"The one and only," he grinned, holding up the shot glass. "I've just got time for another, big guy."

I took the glass out of his hand and set it down. "I came here to question you."

"Well," he said, a bit huffy. "If that's all you want, you'll have to come back to my dressing room. I've got a show to get ready for." He got up and headed away in an instant.

I trailed him backstage to his dressing room, where he took off his bathrobe and hung it on a hook by his lighted makeup table. I'd seen him before, but it was still a little disconcerting to see him in the women's undies he wore beneath the bathrobe.

"What is it you want?" he asked, sitting down and pulling on a pair of nylons.

"Got a few questions, like I said," I told him, standing just inside the door.

"Questions can be fun." He stood and carefully hooked his nylons to his black garter belt, a little smile forming on his lips.

"First," I said. "Did you want Trixie's job?"

"I've got lots of wants." His eyes twinkled. Then he took a dark-blue sequined gown from its hanger beside his makeup table. He stepped into it and pulled the low-cut thing up over his tight corset and around his shoulders. "Help me zip this up, will you?"

"Do it yourself, and answer my question."

"If I can't get zipped up, I can't go onstage, and I certainly can't answer your question."

"O.K., sure, if that's the way you want to play it."

"Just be careful," he told me, a lilt in his voice. "The zipper tends to stick and pinch if you don't take it easy."

I moved behind him and took hold of the zipper. He let out a little sigh as I did so. Small and slim as he was, it was still a pretty tight pull like he said, which suited me just fine. I gave the zipper a solid yank.

"Oww! What are you doing?" He jumped and tried to turn away from me, but I clamped onto his shoulder and held him in position.

"I'm not in the mood for games," I told him. "How bad did you want Trixie's job?" I gave him another pinch with the zipper for emphasis.

"Oww, dammit! Alright, alright ... "

I let go of him this time, and he spun around to face me, rubbing at his back with his right hand.

"Of course I wanted her job," he said. "Why wouldn't I?"

"How far were you willing to go to get it?"

"For heaven's sake," he said. "Is that what all this is about? You think I killed her?"

"You were runner-up in the amateur contest."

"Runner-up, what a laugh." He walked over to his dressing table, took a smoke out of a silver cigarette case, then sat down facing me and crossed his legs as lady-like as any broad I'd ever met. "Look," he told me, threading his smoke into a long, black cigarette holder. "I should have won that contest hands down."

"Sour grapes. So what?"

He lit up and blew out a lazy, fine thread of smoke. "No," he said. "You don't understand. Trixie was a draft-horse compared to me. Thin, yes, but too tall. She had the looks, sure, but she could be gawky in a lot of her moves. Not a real thoroughbred like I am." He gave me sultry, come-hither look and sexily toyed with the front of his low-cut gown like he was about to pull it down and invite me in for some forbidden fruit. "See?" he said archly. "That sure caught your eye, didn't it?"

I felt myself flush. He was right, though I'd never admit it.

"That's what I mean," Adrian went on. "Completely natural, completely feminine in every way. Take you places you've never been, tough guy. Trixie had it some of the time—I have it *all* the time."

"So, why'd he win?"

He smirked. "Take a wild guess, honey."

"You saying the contest was rigged?"

"Let's just say one of the owners might have been sampling the goods."

"Yeah? Which one? Donny or Martin?"

"Don't know." He took his barely smoked cigarette out of its holder and stubbed it out. "That's all I'm saying. I still have to work here, you know."

"Not so fast," I told him. "I want to know—"

"Look," he interrupted, picking up his long-haired wig, which he put on and began to adjust. "Let me give you a tip, honey. If I was you, I'd be talking to Chuck Osbourne. I always thought he had something to do with the murder."

"Osbourne, huh? The guy from the Camlin Hotel?"

"One and the same," said Adrian. "You know him, then?"

"Yeah. Trixie's manager."

"Manager?" Adrian laughed, the long hair of the wig flipping gracefully across his bare shoulders. "And you bought that?"

"Why shouldn't I?"

"Because he's tried to manage every girl in this place, that's why. What a schmuck."

"So he didn't manage Trixie?"

"Just what was between her legs before she got wise to him."

"How do you know that?" I asked.

"Everybody knew it. Chuck didn't take it too well when she ditched him, either."

"Romantically involved, huh? He told me he only had a business relationship with Trixie."

"You get the wool pulled over your eyes pretty easy, don't you sweetie?" Adrian threw me a naughty smile. "There's hope for me, yet."

"That's it for now," I told him. I headed for the door, really wanting a second go-around with Chuck Osbourne.

"Hey," called Adrian. I turned back to face him. "Isn't this where you're supposed to tell me not to leave town or something?"

"Yeah, that's the gist of it. I'll be keeping an eye on you."

He batted his eyes at me. "I certainly hope so."

Chapter

17

I HATED BEING LIED TO. EVEN THOUGH IT was part and parcel of the private dick racket, it still galled me. I'd be sure to let Chuck know exactly how I felt when I caught up to him.

I breezed the couple miles uptown to the Camlin, and found parking on the Seventh Avenue side, back by the cabanas. There were six of them in all, set back on either side of the hotel's large, kidney-shaped swimming pool. Located across from the huge Paramount Theatre, the Camlin had added the cabanas recently, which had given its summer business a real boost. Like little bungalows, the cabanas offered an almost southern California feel to normally gray and wet Seattle during the precious few hot summer months we had each year.

I'd stayed in one when they first opened. Had its own living room, small kitchen, bedroom, and wet bar. Furnished in breezy, bright colors, it was a gas to have a few guests over to party around the pool—felt almost like it was your own swimming pool and you were some carefree, rich mook with vacation digs in Santa Monica or Miami Beach.

Trixie must have been working there when I rented my cabana, I thought. Maybe even brought me cold drinks and a towel or two. Didn't remember seeing him, though. Then again, I doubt I would've imprinted a cabana boy in my memory banks—especially with all the pretty, tanned, and friendly women in scanty swimsuits lounging around the pool.

Right now, in March, however, the cabanas were as deserted as a Florida beach during a hurricane.

I went inside the hotel and asked for Chuck at the front desk. Another joe, a stocky mutt in his mid-thirties, was manning it. He was just sending a young couple off with the bellboy when I walked up.

He acted like I'd said a bad word. "You a cop, too?" he asked.

I had no idea why he asked me that, but I only hesitated long enough to use my most authoritative voice. "Yeah, as a matter of fact, I am."

"Look," he said, leaning over the desk and speaking in a hushed tone. "This might look very bad for the hotel."

"Not my problem."

He sighed. "I can't tell you any more than I told the other detective: I have no idea where he is. I haven't seen Mr. Osbourne since he got away from your officer."

"I see," I told him. "This other detective—where is he?"

"Still in Mr. Osbourne's office, I think. He just went back there a few minutes ago. It's around the corner on the left."

I tipped my hat and walked the direction he pointed. I didn't bother knocking at Chuck's office, just went in like I owned the joint. All alone in the room, and in the process of rifling Chuck's big oak desk, was none other than Lt. Baker.

"Rossiter," he said, as I barged in. "What are you doing here?"

I didn't answer. My focus wasn't on Baker for the

moment. It was on what lay smack in the middle of the neat and tidy desktop: a large, curved blade with a heavy jewel-encrusted handle—undoubtedly a 12th century Saracen dagger.

"That's some knife," I said.

"According to my tipster," said Baker, pulling some letters out of the desk drawer, and fingering through them as he spoke, "it's the knife used to kill that female impersonator."

"No shit?"

"C'mon, Jake," he told me. "What do you know and how do you know it?"

"Where's Osbourne?" I asked.

"On the lam."

"Got outfoxed, huh?"

"Hell, no. It was a simple arrest. Came in, found him at his desk, and found the knife right in his desk drawer just like our tipster said. Of course, Osbourne said he'd never seen it before. Then he went mum, so I sent him over to the station house with Carlson so I could grill him later."

"What happened?"

"Fucking rookie," Baker said with a shake of his head. "Must have put the cuffs on too loose. Said Osbourne slipped 'em and beat it down a stairwell before he could grab him."

"Good help's hard to find."

"Ha-ha," said Baker, with no humor. "My men will get him, though. They're combing the hotel as we speak." He paused, took a closer look at one of the letters.

"Who tipped you?" I asked.

"Anonymous," he said. "Well, well, what do we have here?"

I moved up close to get a look at the letter.

Baker turned away as he took it out of the envelope.

"Share already," I told him. "What am I, just some nameless dick off the street?"

He kept his back to me as he glanced over the letter. After a few seconds, he whistled, then spun around and gave the single piece of stationary a smack with his free hand. "Here's motive. This corks it."

"Gimmee." I jerked it out of his hand and read it for myself.

> *Chucky,*
> *Leave me alone. Quit calling me. I don't want to see you again. Ever!*
> *You were just using me. I should have listened to the other girls.*
> *Trixie*

"Guess you could call that a Dear Johnson letter, huh?" said Baker, cracking wise, which he hardly ever did. He took the letter back from me and returned it to its envelope, adding, "He's our boy, no question."

Just then, one of Baker's uniformed flatfeet hurried into the office.

"Lieutenant! Lieutenant!" he hollered, all out of breath like he'd just run a mile.

"I'm right in front of you, Carlson," said Baker. "You don't need to yell."

"Osbourne's left the hotel, sir!"

"How do you know that?"

"Negro down in the kitchen," he said, trying to catch his wind. "She saw him run out through the delivery door. Martinez and Foley are after him."

Baker shoved the letter into his coat pocket. "Don't just stand there, get outside to the front, see if you spot him."

"Yessir!"

"C'mon, Jake," Baker told me, as his man rushed out. "You game to nab him?"

"More than you think," I said, following him out the door.

As we beat feet past the front desk, Baker told the joe behind it, "Nobody goes into that office, understand?"

"Right," he answered, looking as uncomfortable as the half-dozen guests in the lobby looked surprised at seeing us rush by.

The street in front of the hotel was nearly empty—just a few parked cars, including Baker's black Ford cruiser, the doorman helping an old lady out of her Yellow Cab, and a glimpse of Baker's flatfoot, Carlson, halfway up the block.

"There's your officer," I said, pointing him out to Baker.

"See him yet?" Baker yelled at his man.

"No sir! Nothing!"

"Go block by block! Work in a circle!"

Baker motioned me over to his cruiser, one of the latest radio-equipped models. We hopped in and he got on the radio, put out a dragnet on Osbourne, then juiced the Ford hard enough to give us whiplash.

"Got any idea where he'd go?" Baker asked, as we covered the streets around the hotel in ever widening loops.

"Your guess is as good as mine."

"Shit," he said, swerving to avoid an old jalopy. "I forgot to call the evidence boys in to secure Osbourne's office." He got on the radio again, called a team in, then asked, "What brought you in today, Jake? You got some corroborating info on Osbourne, I'd like to have it."

"I'd talked to him once before, that's all. Told me he was Trixie's manager. I found out otherwise."

"They've got managers?" He laughed, then added, "I shouldn't laugh—they probably make more than I do." Rounding the Paramount off of Olive Way, he asked, "Who told you different? About him not being Trixie's manager, I mean."

"Joe named Adrian. Another female impersonator at the club."

"Guy who came in second in their contest?"

"Yeah. How'd you know that?"

He threw me an insulted look. "What, you think I've just been sitting on my ass? You're not the only one investigating this. We've had our eye on him since day one. Bitchy little bastard."

"Second the motion," I said.

Motoring down Sixth Avenue, couple blocks on the backside of the Camlin, Baker said, "Well, Jake, I'll be damned glad to get this wrapped up."

"Providing your tip was on the level," I told him, not catching sight of Chuck anywhere.

"What do you mean by that?"

"The words *anonymous* and *tip* always make me edgy."

"Hey," he said, blowing through a yellow light. "He's our boy. Got the murder weapon and the motive. I need this closed—take the heat off both of us. I doubt you want your kisser pasted all over the front page again. Sordid bunch of bullshit. This collar will look real good when I'm up for captain next month."

"Just thinking out loud," I said.

"Well, don't. Not unless you've got a damned good line on somebody else for the rap. And frankly, I hope you fucking don't."

"Nope. Got nothing at all."

"Good. End of conversation."

As Baker lit up one of his Old Golds, I noticed more and more squad cars coming into the vicinity and joining the search. The Rat City cops were really good at throwing lot of muscle into an area now that they'd taken more flatfeet off foot patrol and put them into police cruisers. They also seemed to have a little more brainpower than they used to—which wasn't saying much if you considered that not long back they used to hire mostly ex-boxers, ex-wrestlers, and even ex-thugs, since they prized meanness and brawn much more than even a modicum of gray cells.

"Drop me off," I told Baker, when we turned east again on the north side of the Camlin.

"Drop you? Why?"

"Better coverage. Stupid riding around with you when I could be searching on my own. I'll cover some of the back alleys and such on foot—multiply our chances to nab him. Pull over."

Seeing the wisdom of my logic, Baker let me off. "Don't worry," I told him. "I grab him up, you'll be the first to know."

"Better," he said, with a nod of his head, then sped off.

I made a beeline straight back to the Camlin, only four blocks away. We'd been chasing our tails for the better part of fifteen minutes. I had a feeling Chuck was long gone, and I wanted a look-see around his office for myself before Baker's evidence boys got on the scene.

No challenge from the joe at the front desk, I knocked lightly on the door to Chuck's office, then went inside when there was no response.

Locking the door from within, I pawed through all the drawers and filing cabinets to see if there was anything Baker missed. Even though I went through everything with a fine-toothed comb, I came up empty—except for a couple hand-bills that I found folded into the inside pocket of Chuck's overcoat hanging on the coat-tree by his desk. One advertised some place called Mrs. Peabody's School of Dance down in Pioneer Square. The other was for Skipper's All-Night Steam Baths located in the same area of skid road.

I was just thinking that the steam baths might be worth checking out, when I heard the doorknob rattle.

"Shit," said somebody on the other side of the door. "Frigging thing's locked. Get that damned manager back here with the keys."

I stuffed the handbills into my coat, and took my leave via the single, narrow window behind Chuck's desk. The half-story drop into the back alley was a piece of cake, although I twisted my ankle slightly due to the stupid loafers I'd worn rather than my usual oxfords.

I checked the time—pushing 7:00—and decided to swing by the office to see if Heine had nabbed our blackmailer at the bus station drop yet. Whether he had or hadn't, at least I could change into some decent working shoes when I got there.

There were raised voices coming from my office. I recognized them. It was Heine and Miss Jenkins. I was glad she was back on the job, although I was a little nervous about seeing her again after our last encounter.

They went quiet when I walked in. Miss Jenkins, seated at her desk, looked away from me when I entered. Standing across from her, Heine turned and gave me a curt nod.

"What gives?" I asked.

"Just a little difference of opinion," Heine told me.

"Why are you here?" I asked him, noticing nobody else

in the outer office but the three of us. "I sure don't see the blackmailer you were supposed to nab."

Just then, I heard the toilet flush in the bathroom off my adjoining office. A few seconds later, a very familiar face came into the room. A beautiful dame, early twenties, with long, chestnut hair, wearing a light-colored, form-fitting, ultra-stylish dress.

We eyed each other for a moment before I recognized her.

She was none other than the near-naked nymph that I'd first met at Royce Bennington's.

Chapter

18

"MEET DOLORES," SAID HEINE.

"*Dolores?*" I said. The young broad didn't say anything. Just stood there with a dour look on her puss. She started shaking a bit—seemed like she was going to cry. I turned to Miss Jenkins. "Don't tell me this is the same Dolores that you've been—"

"Yup," said Miss Jenkins, her expression just as tart as Dolores's. "None other."

"Well, I'll be damned." I turned back to face the object of my surprise. "It was *you* blackmailing the judge?"

"I caught her red-handed pulling the dough out of that locker," Heine told me. "Had packed bags with her, too, like she was gonna blow town."

"Did Royce Bennington have something to do with this?" I asked Dolores. She kept her lips zipped, so I walked up and towered over her. "Start talking, sister. I'm not in the mood for the silent treatment."

Miss Jenkins jumped up and came around her desk at me. Poking a stiff finger in my chest, she ordered, "Leave her alone."

"Say what?"

Dolores began crying—buried her face in her hands and

shook like she had Saint Vitus Dance—almost made me feel guilty for trying to intimidate her. It bothered Heine, too—he lit a smoke and averted his eyes from her—he always was a sucker for an emotional dame.

"She's been through a lot," Miss Jenkins said, pushing me out of the way and putting a gentle arm around Dolores's shoulder.

"Well, haven't we all?" I said.

"She's had it tough," Miss Jenkins told me. "She's been hiding out at Royce Bennington's because she's been trying to get away from Dennis Diamond."

"And how do you know all that, doll?" I asked her.

"We're friends," said Miss Jenkins. "I'm helping her escape from that hoodlum. That's why I went to the bus station. To see her off."

"What about the blackmail?" Heine asked her.

"I didn't know anything about that," Miss Jenkins told him.

"Please, Mr. Rossiter," Dolores finally spoke up, batting her large, tearful eyes at me. "I'm in danger if I stay. Please help me."

"Hey, Jake," Heine said, glancing at his watch. "You need me anymore? Can you handle this?"

"Yeah, I suppose. I'd kind of—"

"Good," he cut me off. "I'm outta here." Without another word, he blew out the door and was gone.

I watched as the door swung shut—felt a little abandoned—then turned back to the business at hand.

"O.K., Dolores," I said. "I want the straight skinny. Start with the judge. How'd you hatch this blackmail scheme?"

"I didn't." She sat in the chair beside Miss Jenkins's desk, took a hanky out of her purse and dabbed at her welling orbs. "It was Trixie's idea."

"Trixie?" I leaned across the desk at her, my interest more than piqued. "You and Trixie were in on it together?"

"Not actually," she said, drying her eyes. "Say, can I have a drink? I could really use a drink."

"When we're finished," I told her.

She bit her lip and said, "I can't go to jail, Mr. Rossiter. I just can't."

"Keep talking."

"Well," she said. "Trixie and I were friends. I made all her gowns."

"Get back to the blackmail."

"That's what I was getting to," she told me. "Trixie and Judge Torrence had been having an affair, then he broke it off. Poor Trixie was really upset. She told Royce about it, and he felt sorry for her. He told her about a way she could get back at the judge."

"I knew Bennington would be involved somehow," I said. "But why would he?"

Dolores laughed, her tears all dried up now. "Royce likes pulling strings and manipulating people. That's how he gets his kicks. He's twisted."

"So, how'd he help Trixie with the judge?"

"He had photographs. Compromising photographs."

"Yeah, I've heard about those. How'd he get them?"

"He's got secret cameras. They're hidden all over the place."

Miss Jenkins looked utterly shocked. "That's just sick," she said.

"Royce has pictures of everybody who's ever been to his

parties. He's got cameras in his smoking room, as well. That's where he throws his private orgies. He's got thousands of photos. He's got some of me. He's got some of you, too, Mr. Rossiter. Of course, you've got your clothes on, at least in the ones I saw."

Miss Jenkins blushed. I don't think I did, but the news did make me feel a tad hot under the collar.

"Bennington gave these snaps of the judge to Trixie, huh?" I asked.

"That's right," said Dolores. "Trixie thought it would be a good way to make some extra money and get even with the judge."

"And you just went along with that," I said.

"Yeah. Why not? Trixie deserved a break. But then she got herself killed."

"That's when you stepped in."

"Not at first," Dolores said. "But then I thought I could use the photos and make enough money to get away from Dennis." She started sniffling again.

"Why didn't you just walk out the door," I asked her. "Just break off the affair?"

"He's not my lover," said Dolores.

"He's not her lover," echoed Miss Jenkins.

"Yeah? What do you call it, then?"

"Dennis Diamond's queer," Dolores told me.

"Dennis Diamond?" I said. "You sure?"

"Fruity as a fruitcake," she told me. "He wouldn't let me go. Wanted me at his beck and call. Took me everywhere with him. I thought he was dangerous when I first met him. Dangerous and attractive. But I was just window dressing. He never touched me. Not ever! I couldn't take it anymore."

"I don't believe it," I said.

"He's the one who killed Trixie, I'm sure," said Dolores. "He had the hots for her bad."

"Diamond killed Trixie?" I said. "What makes you think that?"

"She was afraid of him," said Dolores. "He was always after her. I don't know anything for certain, but I'm almost positive he did it."

"Why didn't you tell the cops if you had these suspicious?"

"Are you nuts?" she said, looking at me like I was the biggest stoop on the planet. "I've got enough problems with Dennis. If he thought I was a rat, he'd—"

"Then why tell me?" I asked.

"Because I think you can protect me," she said. "Maybe I could trade this information on Dennis for them going easy on me with the blackmail charge. They do that, don't they?"

"Sometimes," I told her. "But from what you've said, your info's nothing but groundless suspicions. Besides, I'm pretty sure another joe did it."

"Who?"

"Guy named Chuck Osbourne."

"Chuck from the Camlin?" She shook her head. "No. I know Chuck. He's no killer. He's a wimp."

"All the evidence points to him," I told her.

The phone rang. Miss Jenkins, nearest to it, picked it up even though it was well past office hours.

"It's for you," she told me. "Lt. Baker."

I grabbed the phone. "Yeah, Baker," I said. "What's up?"

"We just found a body I thought you might be interested in."

"That so? Who's the stiff?"

"Dennis Diamond. Miss Jenkins said you've been talking to him. He was shot. Cop found him out back of the Greyhound bus depot. It's weird—somebody cut off his pinky-finger."

"No shit? Dennis Diamond?" I said. "Dead?"

Dolores burst into tears.

Chapter

19

DOLORES HAD COLLAPSED IN HER CHAIR, bawling her eyes out, Miss Jenkins doing her best to comfort her.

"What's the matter with her?" I asked. "Why's she crying so much?"

Miss Jenkins glared at me. "You don't understand women."

"But she was trying to get away from Diamond," I said. "She hated him. Now the problem's solved."

"That doesn't mean she doesn't still have feelings for him."

"Women," I muttered.

Miss Jenkins bit my head off. "You're so insensitive!"

"O.K. Fine," I said, putting up my palms. I let the air settle a bit as Miss Jenkins pulled Kleenex from the box on her desk and passed tissue after tissue to Dolores. Finally, I asked, "So, what are we going to do with her?"

"You can't take her to the police," said Miss Jenkins.

"Why not, pray tell?"

"They'd arrest her, that's why."

"So?"

At my question, Dolores's crying hit a crescendo.

"Good grief. Aren't you thinking?" Miss Jenkins told me.

"If it went to court, it would all come out about the judge. I doubt he'd want *that*."

"Yeah, guess you're right. We should check with Torrence first," I agreed. "So, got any suggestions? I've got places to be."

"Well, I'll just keep an eye on her," she said.

"What, over at your place?"

"She's in no condition to travel right now. Can't you see that?" She paused, then asked, "Say, how long will you be gone, anyway?"

"A while. Why?"

Miss Jenkins smiled. "I'll just stay here with her, then. Watch her until you get back."

"As long as you don't let her out of your sight."

"Of course not," she said. "We'll decide exactly what to do when you get back."

"Roger," I told her, not liking it, but not seeing any other alternative. Besides, I wanted to get cracking on the one lead I had on Chuck from the handbill I'd picked up at his office. "I'll see you later."

Miss Jenkins didn't say goodbye—just went back to ministering Dolores, who stuck her head up as I left, managed a tiny smile, then continued her hysterics.

I made it to Skipper's All-Night Steam Baths in ten minutes flat. Neither traffic lights nor thoughts of who killed Dennis Diamond slowed me down much. I was champing at the bit to lay my hands on Mr. Chuck Osbourne. Before I'd rung off with Baker, he'd asked me again if I had any idea where Osbourne might be. I'd told Baker no, even though I had a possible lead on him. Trixie's murder was *my* case and I was damned if I going to let any flatfeet, even Baker, one-up me on it. An all-night hang out like Skipper's would be the perfect place to hole up for a joe on the run.

I parked almost right in front of the joint, just south of Yesler on First Avenue. Except for its small neon sign, the entrance to Skipper's was just another hole-in-the-wall in the long line of grimy, pock-marked, turn-of-the-century brick buildings that made up the western edge of skid road. The steam baths butted up against the Union Gospel Mission on the corner, which I found a bit ironic. Right across from it was the Pioneer Square Hotel, which was really no more than a cheap flop house advertising its dismal rooms at fifty cents a night on their large, weathered sign. The flop house would be a good place to canvas if I failed to turn up Chuck at Skipper's.

Skipper's was about what you'd expect on the inside: hot, sweaty, and smelly like a gymnasium, even in the little linoleum-floored area that passed for its foyer. Its walls paneled in yellowed knotty pine, there was nothing in the foyer but a small counter to the left, and a door directly across the room marked STEAM BATH.

A balding joe, in his fifties, wearing a white T-shirt, was reading a newspaper at the counter. I walked up to him. "Four bits," he said, without looking up.

"I'm looking for Chuck Osbourne," I said. "You seen him around tonight?"

He glanced up at me, then back down at his paper. "Four bits, mac."

I pulled out a couple quarters and flipped them on the counter.

"Willy's got towels on the inside," said the joe, his eyes still glued to the newsprint.

I strolled through the door and found myself in another

anteroom. An old geezer with a nicotine-stained, white moustache sat smoking a home-rolled at a table covered with white towels. Right next to him was a double swinging door, its two oval, glass windows all fogged up. To the old gent's left was an open, tile-covered doorway through which I could see a few gunmetal gray lockers.

The guy stopped me as I prepared to go through the swinging door into the steam bath.

"Hold up," he told me. "Can't let you in."

"Why not?"

"Can't go in there with your clothes on."

"I won't be a minute," I said.

"What'd I tell ya, son?" he said, standing up and putting a palm over the big, chrome-plated buzzer on the table. "You don't want trouble, do ya?"

Actually, I wouldn't have minded some trouble, but not with this old coot, let alone whoever his buzzer might summon.

"O.K., dad," I told him.

He smiled, his teeth as yellowed as his moustache. "Here's a towel," he said, handing me one. "Lockers are in there." He pointed to the tiled doorway. "Take #3." He glanced at a small clipboard hanging on the wall behind his table. "Combination for the lock's right-6, left-21, right-18."

There was one other joe changing when I went into the surprisingly large locker room. Jet-black hair, he was in his twenties, and just pulling on his trousers. He smiled at me. I concentrated on getting in and getting out quickly, and found my locker. It was like any other big locker room you'd find anywhere: ringed with maybe forty metal lockers, it had four long benches to sit on while you changed, aligned around the perimeter of the space. The only difference I noted was that, from time to time, while getting undressed in a normal locker room, the thought rarely crossed your mind that somebody may be looking at you the wrong way—in this locker room, however, you *knew* somebody was looking at you the wrong way.

Hat, shoes, clothes, and .45 stuffed into my locker, I got out of there.

The old man nodded at me as I went by him into the steam room wearing only my towel. Inside, in a very large space, the steam was billowing, partially obscuring the view. Like looking into a fog bank, I could make out the nearest forms seated here and there around a big, square pit full of large, hot rocks. A naked joe came out of the fog and poured a round ladle full of water onto the rocks as I watched. The water sizzled and instantly turned to steam as it hit.

The sounds of conversation and men laughing drifted up out of the grayish clouds.

"Not too friendly, is he?" said a joe to another, both lounging naked on a bench across the way. "I think he just likes to look."

The heat felt stifling. Reminded me of the worst jungles Heine and I had fought in during the war.

I had to be careful of the slippery, tile floor as I scouted around the place. I counted ten men in all, none of them Chuck.

An arched, open doorway led into another room. There, a round dipping pool was set into the floor. The air was refreshingly cool. Two guys, who looked to be no more than older teenagers, were immersing themselves in the water as I came in. One of them, with short-cut, blonde hair, stood and gave me a smile and a nod. I couldn't help notice that he had an absolutely chiseled body, looked like a weight trainer, though he wasn't muscle-bound—reminded me of some of the nude Greek and Roman statuary that I'd seen at Royce Bennington's mansion. He struck a pose that looked exactly like Michelangelo's *David*.

I did a fast scan of the area around the pool, saw only a couple older guys who had their eyes glued to the young David, and moved on to the wide hallway that led out away from the pool.

The corridor held ten narrow doors along its length. The first door, on my left, was wide open. The small room behind it was just barely bigger than the single, striped mattress it contained. The next room was also empty. The third, however, was obviously occupied—guttural groans emanating from it.

I wanted to open the door and see if Osbourne might be one of the Romeos.

But I also didn't want to open the door.

I tapped at it instead. "Hey, Chuck," I said, my mouth close to the door jam. "That you, Chuck?"

Sudden silence. A hoarse voice said, "Ain't no Chuck in here. Get the hell away."

I did as ordered. Took two steps down the hall, when a door at the far end came open, and a very large, vaguely familiar form stepped through it. Well over six feet and very husky, he turned his bare backside to me as he said, "That was nice," to whomever he'd left in the room.

Then he closed the door and turned my direction as he put his towel around his waist.

Good God, it was Haggerty, my attorney—rugged out-doorsman, big-game hunter, and man's man extraordinaire.

"Good God," he said, echoing my thoughts when he saw me.

"Haggerty…" I mumbled, walking toward him.

"Jake…" he said, softly, rooted to the spot and trying to force a smile as I closed the distance between us. "You come here, too?" he asked.

"No. I don't," I told him.

An awkward silence followed. We just stood there, holding up our towels, me wondering what he was thinking, and him, undoubtedly, vice-versa.

"Look, Jake," he said, finally. "I—"

"I'm just down here looking for somebody, Haggerty."

"Me too," he said.

"Looks like you found him."

"Judas, Jake, you can't—"

Just then, the conversation neither of us wanted to be having was broken by the sound of very creaky door swinging open down the hall. I turned, caught sight of Chuck Osbourne, towel around his shoulders and bare-ass naked, coming out of a room near the entrance to the pool.

"Hey!" I yelled, making straight for him. "You stay put!"

He did just the opposite—took off at a dead run when he saw me coming. He made it out parallel to the pool before he slipped and went down in a heap. I would've had him right then but, between trying to keep my towel up and run at the same time, I lost my footing on the slippery tiles and took a hard header myself. By the time I got back up, all the joes in and around the pool chirping like a bunch of birds at the unexpected commotion, Chuck was disappearing into the steam room's cloud bank.

I cinched my towel and really turned it on—sprinted after him for all I was worth.

I managed to gain on him quickly. Almost to the stairs, he gave me one desperate, backward glance. I went for the flying tackle, lost my towel in the process, and brought him down, his towel also coming off.

We wrestled. Rolled and flopped and wrestled some more. He was surprisingly strong and slick as a greased pig. It was damned hard to keep a grip on him. This was no wimp, as Dolores had described him—hell, I thought, as he began muscling me around, Chuck must have done a lot of wrestling because he soon got the best of me.

Before I knew it, he'd spun around, his face by my feet, and put a scissors-lock around my neck with both of his legs. Arching his back, he applied the pressure like a giant pair of pliers. I struggled for leverage, but got none as he continued to squeeze the bejesus out of me.

It wasn't that I was much of a wrestler that saved me—it was the proximity of his privates flapping in my face that gave me the will to finally break his hold. I used the only weapon I had in my present position—my teeth—and bit deeply into his inner-thigh.

He yelped like mad, and I managed to slide out from between his vise-like legs. Trying to get to my feet, he grabbed me around the ankles and jerked me back down. I threw a punch as I fell, but he dodged it and somehow got behind me as I struggled back up to my knees. Next thing I knew, he had one powerful arm around me and applied a half-Nelson, painfully pushing my head down, his grip like iron at the back of my neck. Chuck's breath ragged in my ear, his other arm grappled up my side trying to complete the hold and put me in a two-handed full-Nelson. I gave him a sharp elbow to the solar plexus, and he let go.

Whirling around, I thought I had him. But just as I started to unload another punch, he jumped me like a ton of bricks and pinned me to the floor. I couldn't move. He lay on me, his stomach against mine squashing the air out of me as he got hold of my wrists and pushed them up over my head. Try as I might, I couldn't get him off of me.

I put an end to it by bringing my knee straight up into his balls.

Groaning and gasping, he rolled off of me. I looked around for a hand from Haggerty—expected him to help me get Chuck to his feet. But my attorney wasn't anywhere in sight. The big s.o b. had flown the coop.

I managed to get Chuck up, and supported his half-dead weight with one arm around his waist.

I was just glancing around for a towel to put on, when the old geezer towel-attendant hurried into the steam-room with a uniformed cop in tow.

"That's him right there," he said, pointing straight at me. "He's the one who started it all."

Chapter

20

"JUDAS, JAKE," SAID LT. BAKER. "YOU'RE LUCKY that damned photo-hound from the *Star* wasn't there."

"Lucky for him he wasn't." I took another sip of police station coffee. Didn't like it any better than the plain-Jane, bureaucratic décor in Baker's office. "I just hope the flatfoot who picked us up keeps his big yap shut."

"Oh, sure he will." He leaned back in his desk chair and threw me a sarcastic grin. "I mean any cop who nabs two naked joes in a hinky bath house will *never* talk about it."

"Fuck."

"After all, who would they tell?"

"Fine, already, I get the point," I told him.

He laughed. "Just razzing you, Jake. Don't worry, I already had a talk with the officer—asked him to try and keep the scuttlebutt to a minimum."

"Oh, that'll really do a lot of good."

"Anyway," Baker said, pouring us some fresh java from the hotplate on the edge of his desk. "You helped us with a big bust. We got Osbourne, plus vice rounded up all the perverts at Skipper's and shut it down."

"Who'd they drag in?" I asked, thinking of Haggerty.

"Hauled them all in," said Baker. "Lewd conduct. 'Course,

nothing will stick except for a few they caught in the act. Good for all of them to get rousted every now and then— maybe they'll think twice and change their ways."

"Any professionals in the crowd?" I asked. "You know, doctors, dentists, lawyers, those types of people?"

"Not that I'm aware of," he said. "Why do you ask? You run into some folks like that while you were down there?"

"Just curious."

He gave me an odd look.

Detective Sergeant Lawrence stepped into the room. A meaty-faced joe, with half of his right earlobe missing— bitten off by some prostitute's pimp back when he was with vice, so the story went. I only knew him in passing, but understood from Baker that he was a good egg.

"Lieutenant," he said, giving me a sideways glance and a smirk. "You said you wanted to question this Chuck Osbourne yourself. You want me to move him to an inter-rogation room?"

"Thought you would've already done that, Bill," said Baker. "Where is he?"

"Still in the main tank with the rest of those fairies."

"Put him in Number One, I'll be right down."

Sgt. Lawrence nodded and left. I would've said hello, but probably would've gotten some wisecrack that I might not have handled too well.

"Mind if I tag along?" I asked Baker.

"Sure. You've earned it," he said. As we left his office, he added, "But if anybody asks, you were never in on the interrogation. Brass wouldn't like it."

We went down the back stairs—thankfully avoided the main station house area—and went directly to interrogation room number one.

Chuck was pacing the small room's floor when we walked in. The walls were painted the same puke green as the rest of the downtown station house's lower level. Chuck's complexion turned roughly the same shade when he saw me.

"You keep him away from me," he told Baker, taking a couple steps back. "He attacked me."

"You've got nothing to worry about," I told Chuck. "Believe me, I wouldn't want to do it again."

Baker tried his nicey-nicey approach first—smiled and offered Chuck one of his Old Golds. His hands shaking a bit, Chuck took a deep drag off of it after Baker lit it for him.

"So, Osbourne," said Baker, all friendly. "Why not tell us why you did it—it'll go easier you. I could put in a good word to—"

"I've been framed," said Chuck.

"Sure, pal," said Baker.

"I didn't kill Trixie. But I bet I know who did."

"How's that?" I asked.

"I was at the club the night she was murdered."

"We already know that," Baker said. "You were stabbing Trixie."

"No!" Chuck threw his smoke to the floor and squashed it out with his heel. "I went to her dressing room just before she went on stage."

"So you could kill her," said Baker.

"No!"

Chuck ran his hands through his hair. "I just wanted to talk to Trixie and—"

"Then you and Trixie had words. He fired you. He didn't want to have anything to do with you, and you stuck him."

"No."

"Sit down," ordered Baker, pointing to the beat-up oak

table in the middle of the room. Chuck took a seat, Baker sitting tall on the edge of the table nearest him, while I sat across from him.

"Comfortable?" Baker asked Chuck. He didn't wait for an answer, just reached out and slapped him across the kisser. "That's a taste," he told him. "Things are going to get rough for you if you don't start cooperating."

Chuck rubbed at his cheek. "I tell you I was there," he said. "I saw Dennis Diamond in Trixie's dressing room. They were arguing."

"Dennis Diamond, huh?" I said. "What were they arguing about?"

"I don't know."

"What do you mean you don't know?" thundered Baker, winding up like he was going to hit Chuck again.

Chuck winced, said, "I didn't stick around. I left."

"You tell me you loved Trixie, then you see him arguing with this ruthless hood, and you just leave?" I said.

"I ran, O.K.? I was scared to death, so I ran away. Are you satisfied?" Chuck started quietly sobbing. "Dennis Diamond must've killed her. It had to be him."

"If that's what you thought, why didn't you tell the cops?" I asked.

"I was afraid. I heard how vicious he was. I don't think he saw me, but even if he didn't, if he thought I'd accused him—"

"You can cut the act," Baker told him. "This just makes you a suspect in two murders."

"What?"

"You heard me. Dennis Diamond was found dead tonight. You've got motive for both."

"He's dead?"

"Murdered," Baker said. "As if you didn't know."

"I want a lawyer," Chuck told him.

"And I want a million bucks," said Baker. "You'll get a lawyer when I win the Irish Sweepstakes—or right after you've confessed."

"You have to give me a lawyer!" hollered Chuck.

"I'll give you the back of my hand. I'll give it to you more than once, too." Baker stood up, took his coat off and ever so slowly rolled up his shirt sleeves. "Feeling more talkative, now?" he asked Chuck, who had intently watched his every move.

I thought he'd crack for sure. But, instead, he collected himself and stated, calmly, "I want a lawyer."

Baker delivered as promised—gave Chuck the back of his right hand, way harder than the first time he'd smacked him.

Chuck wiped a little blood away from the corner of his mouth. "I still want a lawyer."

Baker redelivered—even harder this time.

"Hit me all you want," said Chuck. "I want a lawyer. It's my right."

Chuck surprised me. Just like he'd surprised me being such a good wrestler. It looked like he'd be a tough nut to crack. I'd been on the receiving end of police questioning enough times, myself. Baker was nicer than most. Still, it brought back unpleasant memories.

"I'm going to go for a while," I told Baker.

"Can't you wait? This won't take long."

I left—didn't answer.

The door to the morgue was open when I got there. Baker had told me he'd put a rush on Diamond's autopsy.

Having to work late, Doc Prescott evidently didn't want to be bothered having to answer the door.

Dennis Diamond's naked body was laying on the steel table when I walked into the autopsy room, Doc Prescott just getting ready to work on him, all his scalpels and such laid out in order. Diamond had a big hole in his chest, and was still wearing all his diamond rings, save one—the one that had been on his right pinky-finger—the same pinky-finger that somebody had cut off.

The smell of whiskey was all over Prescott.

He barely looked up at me. "I'm utterly behind," he said. "Of course, that's nothing out of the ordinary. Neither is it out of the ordinary that you should be involved somehow, Rossiter."

"Sorry, doc. Mind if I have a look?"

"Since you're already doing just that, why ask?"

"Just being polite."

"Don't be polite," he said, "be quick."

I turned Diamond's body over enough to see the exit wound. It was big enough that DiMaggio could've thrown a ball through it.

"Large caliber bullet," I said.

"Exceedingly large."

"Know just how large?" I asked. "Cops find the slug?"

"Yes, as a matter of fact they did," said Prescott. "It's right over here." He went over to the nearby counter, and brought back a big, misshapen hunk of lead in a small cellophane bag. Handing it to me, he said, "They dug it out of a brick wall. It's so mashed up, it's no good at all for ballistics, I'm afraid."

From the heft of it, I gauged it somewhere around a .50 caliber.

"What do you think?" I asked Prescott. ".50 cal. or so?"

"More like a .453 or .458 would be my guess," he said. "Of course, I'm not the ballistics expert, but it's definitely from a very high-powered rifle." He pulled his briar out of his pocket, said, "That all you want? Hope so."

"That's definitely what killed him, right?"

"It would kill me," he said. "Bet it would kill you."

"O.K." I looked closely at the missing pinky-finger's stump—it had been hacked off, was a little ragged, not cut cleanly. "What about the finger?"

"What about it?"

"Well," I said. "Why would somebody do that? Got any ideas?"

"That's your job, Rossiter. Now go away, so I can do mine."

Chapter
21

I ONLY KNEW TWO PEOPLE WHO HAD VERY large caliber rifles. My erstwhile attorney, Haggerty, and Royce Bennington. Since I had nothing else to go on, and since Haggerty lived close, I figured I'd swing by and check his rifle for what it was worth. Besides, I owed him some shit for leaving me holding the bag down at the steam bath. About his turning out queer, well, that was his business.

The moon was out when I rolled up outside Haggerty's place on Magnolia. A large, modern, Frank Lloyd Wright affair overlooking the sound on the hill's southern slope, it was unusual for Seattle, looked almost out of place with the ritzy Magnolia neighborhood's English Tudors, and big Colonials, and such. Must have cost a couple hundred thousand or so to build. He sure made a hell of a lot more dough defending the crooks than I did catching them.

The drapes were closed, but the lights were on when I walked by the tall, aluminum-framed windows leading to the front door. I hit the doorbell, which set off a series of loud chimes. No response, I hit it again; twice this time.

The drapes to the right of the door parted ever so slightly, then slowly closed.

Still left out in the cold, I said to hell with the doorbell and used my fist against the birch door. "C'mon, Haggerty," I yelled. "Open up! I know you're in there."

The door swung open. My attorney was dressed in a Roman toga of all things.

"Good God, Haggerty," I said. "Why the get-up?"

He looked sheepish. "I'm going to a party," he said. "Anyway," he continued. "Sorry about the wait, I thought you might be—"

"The cops?" I said, barging in without an invite. "Considering where I last saw you," I said, striding past him into his brick-floored foyer, "that would be a pretty fair concern."

He closed the door, seemed to shrink to half his size as he replied in a low tone. "Jake, look, that's—"

"Forgotten," I told him. "Except for the part about you ditching me."

"I had to."

"Sure you had to," I said. "Anyway, I got picked up by the cops, and you didn't. I'm happy for you."

He studied me for a minute. "Well, uh, what are you doing here?"

"Just an impromptu visit. By the by, do you know that joe I tackled at Skipper's?"

"Not really," said Haggerty. "His name's Chuck—Chuck Osbourne, I think. I've seen him at the baths a few times and maybe once over at Royce Bennington's, I believe. What did he do? Why do you ask?"

"Killed Trixie, from the looks of it."

"Good Lord." He paused. "Well, that's actually welcome news. That should fully exonerate Donny. Is that why you've come by?"

"I want to see your .453 Winchester. Any heavier rifles, too, if you've got them."

"You want to see my hunting rifles?"

"That's what I said."

"Why?"

"Let's just say I found out one surprise about you today. I want to make sure there aren't any others."

He threw me a quizzical glance. "Fine. Have a seat, I'll bring them out for you."

I sat in one of the Danish-modern type chairs at the side of the foyer, while he went down the hall to retrieve the weapons. Got to say, he looked damned curious in the toga when he walked back carrying the big rifles.

"Here's my .453," said Haggerty, handing the Winchester over.

I opened up the bolt action receiver. It had a shell in the chamber. I took out the monster cartridge and I gave the chamber a good sniff. No residual smell of gun powder, I turned it on end and smelled the muzzle. No odor of gun powder there, either.

"I haven't fired it for a while," Haggerty told me.

"Roger." I took the other rifle from him. Model I wasn't familiar with—his favorite elephant gun, according to Haggerty. It was the same story. Hadn't been fired recently.

"That one hasn't been fired since my last safari with Royce Bennington," he said.

"Bennington, huh? How long ago was that?"

"Six months. Say, do you want to tell me why you're doing this?"

"Joe named Dennis Diamond's laying in the morgue with an elephant gun-sized hole in him."

"Diamond, huh?" He carefully leaned the rifles up against the wall. "The hood who works for Rollo Mudd?"

"Yeah. You know him?"

"No. I defended his boss once, that's all."

"Small world."

"You think *I* had something to do with Diamond's murder?"

"Didn't say that," I told him. "I'm just eliminating any obvious possibilities."

"I see." He frowned. "Well, Jake, old top, I must say I'm a little insulted."

"Just business. You, of all people, should understand that."

"Yes, well," he said, "if that's all you came for, I need to finish getting ready for Royce's Bacchanalia. Only happens once a year, and I don't want to be late."

"That's right, it is tonight," I said, recalling the date from the invitation I found.

"How do you know about it?" Haggerty asked.

"I've got my ways," I said. "As a matter of fact, I may crash the party."

"Can't get in without a costume, Jake."

"That all right," I said. "I might just go dressed as a private detective."

Before I hit the Bacchanalia, I swung back to the office to see how Miss Jenkins was doing. The place was empty when I got there—no Miss Jenkins or Dolores—just a note saying that they went to get the rest of the pictures. I didn't know what the deuce they meant, then it registered when I noticed the dozen or so snapshots laying off to the side of Miss Jenkins's desk: a bunch of black & whites of Judge Torrence in all his glory—naked as a newborn and committing a multitude of unnatural acts with Trixie and at least three different joes—*and* a few photos of him frolicking with *all four* joes at once.

So, they were off getting the last of Dolores's blackmail photos. Fine by me, that'd be one less thing to worry about when it came time to settle accounts with Dolores.

I rolled up to Bennington's at half-past seven. His wing-ding was already going full bore. There not being a single spot to park, even in his long drive, I wheeled the Roadmaster off in the grass where at least a dozen other drivers had put their rides

As I walked up to his mansion, three joes came racing pell-mell down the joint's wide steps. The two in the lead, about in their mid-twenties, were dressed like Haggerty in Roman togas. The guy chasing them, roughly the same age, was dressed, of all things, like Uncle Sam: top hat, striped pants, blue coat, and a gray goatee.

All of them giggly and laughing like they were hopped up on something, Uncle Sam thrust out an arm, pointed at them and shouted, "*I want you! I want you!*"

The other two shrieked with delight and yelled, "No! No!" then threw their arms up and took off with renewed vigor. Uncle Sam chased them down the length of the mansion before disappearing around the corner.

The front door of the place was wide open. I went right in. The sounds of cool jazz music drifted down the hallway across the wide, mosaic-floored foyer.

The old butler stood in the hallway. He was dressed like Ali Baba from the forty thieves—complete with red silk turban, red-sashed, blue satin baggy pants, curled-toed golden slippers, and a small, silver-threaded vest that was open in the front, revealing his bare, potbelly and wizened, white-haired chest. He held a silver tray full of jewel-encrusted, golden goblets.

"Mr. Rossiter," he said, a little startled when he saw me. "You need a costume."

"I'm wearing it." I pointed at my street duds with both hands. "Where's Bennington?"

"I imagine he's somewhere in all the revelry," said the butler. "I haven't seen Mr. Bennington in quite some time, actually."

"I'll find him."

As I brushed by the old goat, he offered me one of the goblets filled with some kind of blood-red wine. I passed and kept going. I didn't really care if I found Bennington or not—not until I'd had a chance to give his rifle collection the once-over. It was a long shot that he killed Dennis Diamond. I couldn't think of any motive for it. But he was the only other joe I knew, besides Haggerty, that owned the type of weapon involved. Besides, the fact that he owned the knife that'd killed Trixie was coincidental. And in my business, no matter how mundane they might seem, coincidences were always suspect.

The main living area was packed with partygoers. The tuxedo-clad, negro jazz trio hit their licks, heavy on the lead sax, while I squeezed through the forty-odd folks in the enormous, high-ceilinged living room. Many were in togas, complete with laurel head-wreaths, but a lot were in other costumes, too—including one amorous pair dressed as Little Bo Peep and her sheep, and a joe across the way wearing a medieval executioner's outfit, complete with a black skull cap, a half-face mask, and a large and menacing headsman's axe.

In the center of the milling room stood the big fountain spilling over with champagne that Miss Jenkins had mentioned, a number of folks bellied up to it and quaffing their fill by using the many tall gold and silver cups that were arranged around its circumference.

Keeping an eye out for Bennington, I made my way through the crowd and got several odd looks because of my attire—which was rich considering I was the only normal joe in the joint.

I'd barely gotten to the other side of the room, near the corridor that led to Bennington's study, when a firm hand grasped my shoulder from behind.

I spun around, ready for anything, and came face to face with the medieval executioner.

Half covered with the black mask, something about the bottom half of his mug looked vaguely familiar.

"Rossiter," he said in a whisper. "What are you doing here?"

It was Judge Torrence.

"Judas," I said. "What are you doing here?"

"Shhhh!" he told me. "Not so loud."

He drew me into an unoccupied corner where we stood beneath a large, old, oil painting of the Greeks' Trojan Horse left outside the gates of Troy.

"I thought you were laying low," I told the judge, keeping my tone hushed.

"Well, I was," he answered, still looking scary as hell in his costume even though I knew his true identity. "It's just that ... Royce's Bacchanalia only happens once a year."

"Certainly an apropos outfit, your honor," I said. "I sure hope I never end up in your courtroom."

"So, what are you doing here?" he repeated, his voice more like a hiss this time around. "You're supposed to be out trying to catch the blackmailer."

"Already did. Caught the culprit red-handed."

"You did?" he said out loud, his lips curling into a smile.

"Yeah, but there's one small hitch that we'll have to discuss."

"Oh, no..."

We were interrupted by a couple toga-boys who edged up to us in an obvious come-on attempt.

"Go away!" bellowed the judge. "We're busy."

Like any sensible joes confronted by an angry executioner, they were gone in a flash.

"Don't get your bowels in an uproar," I told the judge. "It's not that big a problem. We recovered all the money. You've just got to decide if you want to press charges or not."

"What about the photos?" he asked, coming nose to nose with me. "Did you get them, too? All of them?"

"My partner's picking up the rest of them right now."

"Thank the Lord," he said, backing off and stroking his chin with his free hand. "No. No prosecution. I can't have the publicity. Just put the fear of God into the culprit. Who was it?"

"Girl named Dolores Carver."

"Who the devil is she?"

"Trixie's seamstress," I told him. "She apparently helped herself to the photos after Trixie was killed."

"That snip. Rotten bitch. The gall of some people."

"O.K.," I said. "Soon as Miss Jenkins gets the last pictures, we'll let Dolores off the hook. Don't worry, I'll make sure she doesn't bother you again."

"Good. I feel so relieved." He let out a great, big sigh. "I'll mail you your bonus money. We won't be seeing each other again."

"Fine by me," I said, glad to have been able to handle

the business about Dolores, but now wanting to get back to Bennington's study.

"Goodbye, Mr. Rossiter." He extended his black-gloved hand. We shook and went our separate ways.

Nobody bothered me walking down the trophy-lined hall to Bennington's private study. It was as dimly lit as ever, and the eyes of the mounted, big-game heads tracking my movement were as eerie as my first trip through here. I never liked the feeling that I was being watched even though I did a lot of watching, myself, as a private dick.

The door was locked. I took out my skeleton keys and made short work of it. Once inside, I flipped the switch to the pair of wall sconces on either side of the door, figuring that would be plenty of light to work by, but not enough to attract attention. Then I went directly to his gun collection at the far end of the room.

His .453 Winchester was clean. Likewise a pair of Remingtons. The last rifle of large caliber, a finely tooled Italian Barretta, had also not been fired recently.

Scratch Bennington, I thought.

As I was going by the desk on my way out, I noticed a jumble of photographs lying on the floor next to it. I hadn't noticed them on my way in, intent as I was about the rifles. Looked like somebody had dropped them there.

I went and picked them up—just about fell over when I saw their subject matter—a wild and crazy Miss Jenkins whom I'd never met.

I couldn't believe it.

Miss Jenkins, in Bennington's huge living room at the head of a hopping Conga line, her curly locks flying, one hand on her hip, shaking it like Dorothy Lamour and Mae West put together. Miss Jenkins, at the edge of the champagne fountain, giving some slick-headed Lothario a drink from one of her high-heeled shoes, and laughing like there was no tomorrow.

It got worse.

Miss Jenkins in Bennington's hookah-room, reclining in the pillows, her eyes glazed, puffing on his big water pipe. Miss Jenkins laying on a large bed, her mouth slack, one shoe kicked off, her dress loose around her shoulders. Miss Jenkins and Dolores, both lying on the same bed, both in the same state as the former photo.

It got even worse.

Miss Jenkins, one shoulder bare, one nylon loose and falling down, arm in arm with Dolores, who was only in her undies, her pearly-whites flashing as she had trouble keeping Miss Jenkins on her feet.

It got much worse.

Miss Jenkins, clad only in her dark panties and garter belt, tossing her brassiere aside as if doing a striptease. Miss Jenkins, merrily prancing like a pony, *stark naked*!

There were more, but I stopped there.

Sonofabitch. I don't know if jealous was the word to describe how I felt when I saw those damned photos. But if it wasn't, the word flabbergasted was also high on the list.

Then it hit me.

Miss Jenkins and Dolores had said they'd gone off to get the rest of the pictures. I'd assumed they were talking about the ones of Judge Torrence. Now I realized it was these.

Just a little earlier, Dolores mentioned that Bennington took secret photographs of all his guests. Miss Jenkins hadn't known that until tonight. She sure as hell would have wanted to get these back.

By God, Miss Jenkins and Dolores must've been here.

Maybe got caught in the act of retrieving the photos and dropped them.

But where were they now? Miss Jenkins wouldn't have left those pictures of herself without a fight. She was too damned feisty.

I stuffed all the photos of Miss Jenkins into my sport coat's inside pocket. Throwing caution to the wind, I flipped all the lights on and paced the room looking for some clue. Any clue.

I prowled the room but nothing seemed out of place. Then I spotted it. A shiny tube of lipstick laying at the edge of the wall-length row of bookshelves on the right side of the study. I scooped it up and pulled off the cap. Bright red, with an underlying darker tinge, it was Miss Jenkins's shade, I was sure of it. But what was it doing over here?

The bookcases.

Same bookcases with the secret door in them that Dolores, the nymph, had come through when I first met her.

I remembered that the door was somewhere near the middle of them. I pushed and prodded looking for the hidden locking mechanism. No luck, I did it all over again. As my temper built, I shoved, hit, twisted and kicked the damned shelves. That did the trick: a small square in the bookcase's bottom panel folded inward as my oxford made contact with it.

A bank of books swung open revealing a pitch-black passageway. A few feet inside, just at the periphery of the light, lay a small, silver compact. Beside it, was an open pack of Blackjack chewing gum. Miss Jenkins's brand.

And a few drops of blood, still wet, beside the gum packet.

I checked the .45 in my shoulder holster and stepped into the darkness.

Chapter

22

THE SOUNDS OF THE SOIREE EBBED AND flowed around me as I navigated the jet-black passageway by the light of my Zippo. As the passage twisted and turned, the laughter and music got softer, then louder.

Here and there, I came to small, open doorways that led into tiny rooms off the passage. Each contained still cameras mounted on tripods and set up in front of peepholes or what must have been one-way mirrors. The first one I looked through viewed an empty bathroom. The second had a panoramic view of Bennington's living area, where the party was going full blast. I lingered a minute there, didn't spot Bennington or Miss Jenkins in the crowd, then kept going as the camera whirred and clicked.

I moved the next few cameras back and checked out the action—somebody dressed as the Big Bad Wolf was eating Little Red Riding Hood in some kind of playroom, and a joe in diapers lying on a bed while a pretty dame wearing nothing but a frilly apron changed them for him.

I'd seen more than enough, when the passage took a hard turn and got to a stairwell. I could go up or I could go down.

I looked around for any more traces of blood that might point the way. Finding none, I chose to go up the stairs.

The Zippo was getting hot in my hand as I passed a couple more alcoves with cameras in them. I checked both of them to see if Miss Jenkins was anywhere in view. Nada. Just some more perverted goings-on.

If Bennington had hurt Miss Jenkins, I was going to hurt him. Then hurt him again.

I went a long stretch with no more alcoves or cameras. Finally, I came to a door with a large drop-latch on it. Hearing muffled voices on the other side, I lifted the latch and popped through.

I found myself in Royce Bennington's Arabian hookah-room. Bennington, dressed like some Arab sheik, lounged on large, colorful pillows across the room from me. Two other people were sharing the hookah with him, one dressed like Henry the Eighth, the other in a hairy gorilla costume.

Bennington barely raised an eyebrow when he saw me.

"Why, Mr. Rossiter," he said, taking the hookah's snake-like smoking stem out of his mouth. "I had no idea you were joining us this evening," he went on pleasantly, rising to his feet.

"Cut the crap," I said, side-stepping the two folks in front of me and moving a pace toward him. "I want to know—"

"Look, friends," Bennington told his pals, pointing at me with a flourishing gesture. "He's got the most original costume of the evening. He's come as a private detective."

The one in the gorilla outfit scanned me appreciatively. "He looks just like Sam Spade in the movies."

"Or Philip Marlowe," said King Henry. "Do you have a gun?" he asked me. "Can I see it?"

"Where's Miss Jenkins?" I barked at Bennington.

Grinning, Bennington threw me a wink. Then he turned, yanked back part of the hanging tapestry behind him, and disappeared through yet another damned secret door.

I charged after him, knocking over the hookah as I went. "Oh, they're play-acting, too!" exclaimed one of Bennington's companions as the tapestry flapped shut behind me. "It's wonderful!"

I could hear Bennington running ahead of me in the darkness. He giggled insanely as he ran, like this was all really just part of some silly game. I was deadly serious and struggled to cut his lead. But I couldn't see a fucking thing, kept bumping into walls, tripping, and couldn't catch up.

I ran pell mell into some kind of railing—half knocked the wind out of myself and almost went down. I got my balance and finally thought to light my Zippo again. It was the railing of a metal, circular staircase that had caught me. I heard footfalls on the grated, metal steps somewhere far below.

Down I went—down, down and down the tight, winding stairs—the flame of my wind proof Zippo dancing and blowing all about.

I must have descended several stories by the time I reached the bottom, my head reeling from the fast and continuous, spiral turns.

It was a dead end. There wasn't anywhere to go except through another latched door that I spotted off to my right. I opened it up and went through.

I'd entered a big, dimly lit room. About a dozen people in various costumes were all crowded together, facing away from me, at the far end of it. As my eyes adjusted to the low light, I saw that the room had stone walls, a matching, roughly hewn stone floor, and—Damnation! The joint was a dungeon. It was set up like a medieval torture chamber with chains and vicious bullwhips hanging on the walls around me. An iron maiden and a rack stood off to the sides of the room halfway down to where the crowd had started jostling into each other, as if they were all trying to be the ones at the front.

I heard a voice coming from on the other side of the crowd.

"Oww! Stop that! If you touch me again I swear I'll kill you! Let me loose! Can't you see this isn't a game?"

I recognized that voice. It was Miss Jenkins! Anybody hurting her, I'd bust some heads.

"Stop! Stay away from me!" she screamed.

I ran down and shoved through the clutch of people, knocked them out of the way like so many bowling pins.

When I reached the front, I couldn't believe my fucking eyes.

Miss Jenkins was locked in a barred cage, like a big, wrought-iron bird cage, that hung down from a tall, black pole set into the stone floor. Beside her, gagged, Dolores was chained to the wall by her wrists and ankles. A sign, fastened between them, read: WE WERE BAD GIRLS—WE NEED CHASTISEMENT. Everybody in the crowd had little riding-crops in their hands.

When I came to my senses, two skinny joes in gladiator outfits were poking at Miss Jenkins with their crops. "Isn't this neat?" one asked the other.

Miss Jenkins spotted me as I rushed forward. Her eyes wild, she opened her mouth big as a barn door, but only one word escaped it. "Jake!"

I knocked both gladiators on their asses. All the other

people, including a couple good looking women, gasped and drew back.

"Hey!" said one of the gladiators, picking himself back up.

"Don't worry, doll," I said, fumbling with the lock to her cage. "I'll get you out of here."

"This is terrible," she mumbled, her cheeks flushed bright red, as I struggled with the lock. "Just terrible."

Dolores made a series of grunting noises through her gag.

"Why'd you do that?" asked the other gladiator, pawing at me as he stood up.

I shoved him back. "Lay off!" I shouted. "All of you!" I yelled at the crowd in general.

"Spoilsport," said somebody in the throng.

"Hell," I told Miss Jenkins. "I can't get this thing open. Did Bennington do this? He must have a key."

"Yes, that rat!" she exclaimed. "But get me loose! Try your skeleton keys for God's sake."

In the heat of the moment, I'd forgotten about them. I tried them every which way, but they didn't work in the thing's ancient lock.

"No use, doll. I've got to get after Bennington. I'll be back."

She looked like a little kid at her first Frankenstein movie, her eyes bulging. "You're not leaving me like this!" she shrieked.

"No choice."

I turned to the crowd, who'd edged closer while I was trying to help Miss Jenkins. "If anybody touches her before I get back," I warned them, displaying the .45 in my shoulder holster, "I'll shoot the shit out of you!"

"As if that's a real gun," said somebody.

"*It is!*" Miss Jenkins yelled as I went out through the dungeon's main door.

I hit the hall at a fast clip—could only go left as I was at the end of the corridor—figured I was in the mansion's basement since the hallway's walls and floor were made of the same stone as the dungeon itself.

Damn, I was afraid I'd lost Bennington. He'd probably gone into some other secret passageway that I'd never find.

A little ways up ahead, I came to a bamboo-covered doorway. The sound of drums throbbed behind it.

Not knowing what to expect, I pushed the door open and went inside.

It was a bar. A bar like you'd expect to find in the South Seas. Lazy, teak ceiling-fans pushed around the smoke from the joint's costumed guests, who lounged in rattan chairs and sipped their drinks at some of the bamboo tables. Decorated with palm fronds and tropical flowers, the joint had a grass mat floor and a tall, stand-up, bar counter at the back of it that was made from thick, dull yellowish pieces of bamboo. The wall behind the counter was covered with layers of thin, light brown reeds, upon which hung primitive spears and blow guns and shields painted in geometric patterns. A sign exactly in the middle of the wall read: THE WILD MAN OF BORNEO LOUNGE.

I didn't see Bennington, but I did see something that piqued my curiosity. Hanging down along the bar from the ceiling, were small, brownish-black things that turned in the breeze of the fans. I moved in closer—they were, by God, a bunch of shrunken heads. Real shrunken heads, like the headhunters took in Borneo and Java. They dangled by their long, shiny, black hair, each Brazil-nut-hued face a native tribesman in miniature. Except for their eyes, which were rudely sewn shut, you could almost imagine they were still alive, hunting through the jungle with spears and blow-guns to take heads of their own. They were gruesome, yet fascinating. But I never could shake the hinky feeling I got when I saw one: scuttlebutt had it during the war that a few of our own troops had been taken by headhunters.

I'd just gone up to the bar for a closer look-see, when I took note of the two men sitting part way down the bar counter. Dressed like Roman senators, they were embracing each other, and carrying on and kissing like a couple teen-agers in heat. They broke it off and turned to face me when I reached the counter.

It was Donny and Martin.

"Jake," said Donny, all smiles.

"Hiya, Jake," said Martin.

"What gives?" I was really surprised. "I thought you two were on the outs."

"Not any more," Martin happily announced, patting his partner on the knee. "We're getting back together. Thanks, Jake. Thanks for everything."

"And how," said Donny, reaching over and vigorously shaking my hand. "You caught the real killer and got me cleared with the cops, too."

"How do you know about that?"

"Haggerty told us," he said.

"Haggerty?"

"Yes," said Martin. "We ran into him here at the party, and he told us all about Chuck Osbourne."

"What a relief," Donny said. "It's made us realize just how important our relationship is. That's easy to forget if you're playing around."

"Not anymore," said Martin. "We're going to make it work this time. A real Scout's effort."

"I'm glad for you," I said. "But I've got to go."

"Stay and celebrate with us," said Donny. "We'll buy you a drink."

"Can't. Miss Jenkins is in a jam. I've got to find Royce Bennington. Seen him?"

"No."

"What's the matter with Miss Jenkins?" Martin asked.

"She's locked in a cage in Bennington's damned dungeon."

"What?" Donny asked, utterly incredulous. "Dungeon? Here? I can't believe it."

"Believe it," I told him. "I couldn't get her out. Bennington has the key, and I've got to find him but quick."

"Can we help?" asked Martin.

"Yeah, you can. Go down there and keep her company 'til I get back. Keep the damned spectators away from her."

"Don't worry," Martin said, pulling Donny to his feet. "We'll take care of it."

As they took off out of the bar, Donny asked him, "Where's this dungeon at? I've never been there before."

"I have," said Martin.

"*You have?*" Donny stopped in his tracks, seemed more upset than surprised.

"Hurry up," Martin said, shoving him out the door. "I'll explain later. You're going to enjoy it."

I turned to the joe tending bar, who was bare-chested in a grass skirt and sported a big, bone necklace. "Hey, bud," I said. "Have you seen—" I broke off when I saw the three large jars behind him that sat under the bar's wide mirror. The nearest one contained pickled eggs, which was common to a lot of watering holes. What the next one held, I don't know—it was the last one that really caught my eye. There was something sitting at the bottom of it—a small, gray-pink thing only a couple inches long. I craned my neck toward it, and a glint from the jar brought me to full attention.

"That jar," I told the bartender, in no uncertain terms. "The one on the end. Gimme it. Right now."

Puzzled, he did as ordered—reached back and handed me the jar.

What I held gave me the chills.

A severed, human finger. Fresh, not dried up.

A pinky finger, to be exact.

A pinky finger with a huge, diamond ring on it.

Dennis Diamond's missing finger.

Chapter

23

"WHAT'S THE MATTER WITH YOU, MISTER?" asked the bartender.

I set the jar down—didn't respond.

Royce Bennington must've killed Dennis Diamond. Had to. Everything else paled by comparison, except, maybe, Miss Jenkins in the dungeon. This had turned downright dangerous.

"You know where Bennington's at?" I asked. When the barkeep said *no*, I addressed all the other patrons in the joint. "Anybody in here know where Royce Bennington is? Anybody?"

Nobody volunteering his whereabouts, I was about to blow the joint, when the door to the bar opened and in walked Bennington himself and his old butler. They froze just inside the door when they saw me—glanced nervously at the jar on the bar counter. Unfortunately, I also froze for a second.

And that's all it took. I'd barely thought to yell at him and reach for my gun, when Bennington blasted back out the door. The butler stayed put to run interference for him. I bowled the codger over with ease, but he slowed me just enough that, when I hit the hall, his boss was history.

Where the fuck was he? What the fuck was on his mind? He had to know I was on to him. Where the hell would he go?

Miss Jenkins!

I raced back to the dungeon, half expecting to see Bennington holding a knife to her throat.

No. She was still in her cage, Donny and Martin standing guard. Bennington was nowhere in the crowd.

"Have you got the keys?" Miss Jenkins yelled when she saw me.

"No!" I yelled back, then ran out into the hall again.

Think. Think. What would he do if he knew the game was up? Where would he go?

I knew what I'd do—I'd get myself some kind of weapon. And Bennington had a whole arsenal in his study.

I had two ways to get there. Maybe waste time finding my way upstairs to the main floor, then go back through the house to his study, or hit the secret passage that'd ended down in the dungeon. It went clear to his smoking room at the top, but the adjoining passage from there led right back down into the study.

I chose the secret passageway—ran into the dungeon again to access it.

"*Now* have you got the keys?" yelled Miss Jenkins.

"No!"

She was really shaking her cage as I gained entrance through the secret door. I lit my windproof Zippo and took off up the dark passage as quick as I could fly.

Bennington could be in here lying in wait to blindside me, I thought, while scurrying up the twisting, circular staircase. He could be hiding anywhere along the way.

Fine. If he tried it, I'd just get my hands on him that much sooner.

My radar working overtime in the dark, I made the smoking room without incident, and startled a new group of smokers around the hookah as I charged through them and got myself into the other secret passage.

It was faster going than my first trip through it, even with staying alert for any surprises. I took off the safety and cocked the trigger on my .45. It had a light trigger-pull and I always kept an extra round in the chamber. Gave me an additional shot if I ever needed it.

How Royce Bennington had taken out a tough hoodlum like Dennis Diamond, I didn't know. The world was just full of surprises. Why he'd rubbed him out, I also didn't know. But I'd be sure to beat it out of him if I didn't have to kill him first.

I took it easy down the flight of stairs leading to the main floor, thinking that Bennington might be lurking under them. Safe at the bottom, I retraced my earlier steps and ended up outside the hidden door to his study.

I was sure this was the one. I put my ear to it and listened intently.

Not a sound from the other side. Nothing.

If he was in there, he was due for a shock coming though his own damned secret doorway.

I flung the door open and moved inside in one motion.

Well, almost inside, as it turned out.

I was halfway through the door, my gun extended and ready, when the damned thing slammed back into me. It knocked me backwards a pace and caught my gun-hand at the wrist, smashing it between the door and the doorjamb. I lost my grip and the Colt went off as it fell from my hand.

I immediately slammed the door back open with all my weight. Charging through, I found myself face to face with the muzzle of my own .45.

"You shot my rhino," said Bennington, stepping back a bit and pointing to the stuffed black rhino head mounted high on the wall behind him. A big hole was clearly visible just below the beast's left eye.

"Too bad you weren't up there dusting it or something," I told him, trying to shake some life back into my mostly numb and tingling right hand.

He smiled. Still in his full Arab regalia, he took off his headdress and tossed it aside, saying, "You're a most ill-mannered guest, yet highly entertaining. I quite enjoy having you around, Mr. Rossiter. I haven't had this much fun since I shot Dennis Diamond."

I didn't respond—had my eye on the racks of guns and various blades on the other side of the room.

"Aren't you the least bit curious why I killed him?" Bennington asked.

I still held my peace—wondered if there was any way I could get to any of the weapons before he shot me.

"I'd think you'd be dying to know," said Bennington. "Even if you thought you were just about to die." He snickered at his own joke.

"O.K., shoot," I told him.

"Shoot," he laughed. "Shoot, you say. That's very clever. You have such a quick wit, Mr. Rossiter."

"If you're going to tell me your story, just spit it out." I wanted to hear it, sure, but I hoped it was a long one just to try and buy more time.

"By all means," he said, doing a fair imitation of an Arab-style bow, complete with the circular hand-flourish. "But it will cost you."

"What do you mean?" I asked, edging left and slightly forward toward the weapons just to see if I could get away with it.

"Back, Mr. Rossiter. Back," he ordered, wagging the Colt at me. I did as requested. "I know you'd like to get at those weapons." He grinned, said, "Have patience, you'll get your chance."

I wondered just what he meant by that. But before I had a chance to ask, he said, "Where were we? Oh, yes. We were talking about the price of my story. Well, to begin, I must compliment you on your partner, Miss Jenkins. She's quite a little vixen. Do you know that she managed to knee me in my privates before I knocked her unconscious?"

"You put Miss Jenkins in a cage for that?"

"She was naughty," he told me. "Almost as naughty as Dolores for trying to leave the sanctuary I've been graciously providing her. I couldn't very well let Dolores flee my castle keep, now could I? I've grown very fond of my little nymph." Bennington chortled and chuckled for a moment. "Don't worry, I'm only keeping them in the dungeon for the duration of the party. They make a nice added attraction." He paused. "No, strike that: Dolores must do penance a while longer, maybe quite a while longer. As to Miss Jenkins, well, I'm really only keeping her caged until I decide what to do with her."

"You crazy sonofabitch. I oughta—"

"Tush, tush," he said, sticking the .45 at me. "Your Miss Jenkins kept using the threat of your potential arrival as if it would frighten me. Poor dear didn't know that I desired your presence. Of course, I never imagined that you'd stumble across the little trophy I took from Mr. Diamond." He took a deep breath and sighed. "Most unfortunate. Anyway, we should get back to the original question."

"Which was?" I asked.

"You wanted to know why I killed Dennis Diamond. And I said I'd tell you the story but the cost would be high," he said. "Can you afford it, Mr. Rossiter?"

"I'll do my best," I told him. "But I'm on a bit of a budget."

"Clever as always, aren't you?" He smiled that warm smile again that I'd come to really distrust. "Very well. We'll have some sport."

Keeping the gun trained on me, he backed across the room, took a brief gander at his weapons collection, then said, "I'm sure you're an expert hand with firearms. So am I. So, we'll leave those out of the contest. You see, Mr. Rossiter, I don't want to kill you as much as I want to simply best you. After that, who knows? We'll just go where a fair wind takes us."

He took a few steps over to where all his swords and knives were mounted, shifted the .45 to his left hand, and deftly plucked one of two, crossed rapiers from the wall. He flexed it, then pointed it at me. "How are you with a rapier, Mr. Rossiter?"

"I'd prefer pistols at ten paces," I told him.

"That's what I thought. But you don't have one, and I do. This will be much more interesting than me just shooting you, don't you agree?" He tossed the rapier over at my feet, stuck the .45 into the sash at his waist, and grabbed the other rapier off the wall. "Don't just stand there," he told me, slowly advancing, his thin blade straight out at me, its point making tiny circles in the air. "*En garde!*"

I scooped up the rapier he'd thrown me. My right hand was tingling like hell, so I switched the blade to my left. I wished I'd taken fencing at school, but they don't give fencing lessons at the orphanage, so I backed away as Bennington continued to run his mouth.

"The rules of the game are very simple," he told me. "I'll give you an answer to a question with each *touché*."

"How will you answer questions if you're dead?" I asked, whipping my rapier wildly in front of me while backing toward his desk at the other end of the room.

"Good question." His left hand behind his back, he effortlessly stepped way out on his right foot, extended his body and pricked my left shoulder with the tip of his blade. Surprised the hell out of me—he'd stuck me from a good twelve feet away. It barely penetrated my skin, but I yipped and knew I'd have to keep more distance between us if I could.

"*Touché!*" he exclaimed, stopping in place. "See? Now you get an answer to a question."

"Oh, that's how it works, huh?" I said, glancing about for anything else to use to defend myself.

"Indeed. Works both ways. Only fair, don't you think, considering your level of skill?"

"Really big of you," I said. "O.K. Since I don't want to get stuck more than once, let's go for the brass ring: why'd you kill Dennis Diamond?"

"He'd threatened me."

"About what?"

"Ah-ha!" he said, coming at me again. "That's another question!"

Damnation. I about fell over myself trying to stay away from him. I tried to think of his thrusts like a boxer's jab—

that I knew well—but only managed to parry his blade once before getting stuck another time, this one in my left thigh—just another pinprick, but it smarted.

Again, he held his ground. "He forced his way into my house the other day. Said he'd looked everywhere for Dolores, and he thought she was hiding out at my place."

"What did you do?"

"Yet another question!" Bennington came at me quick. I'd better be more careful asking questions, I thought, as I tripped at the foot of his desk and fell backwards in a heap.

He drew a speck of blood from my cheek with his damned, masterful blade. Then he stepped back while I scrambled to my feet and put the desk between us.

"I told Mr. Diamond to leave," he explained. "I also told him that if he ever bothered me or Dolores again, I'd reveal his homosexuality to his mobster friends. That would undoubtedly make his life 'tough' as they say."

"That's when he threatened to kill you."

"That's a question!" He lunged at me over the desk.

"Not a question!" I screamed at him, side-stepping his thrust. "Only a statement of fact!"

He held his position. "Yes, it was, wasn't it? Very crafty Mr. Rossiter. Kudos to you."

I grabbed the letter opener off his desk and threw it at him. Would've been nice if it had stuck in this chest, but the damned unbalanced thing just bounced off of him.

"Well," he said, rubbing at his breastbone, then locked eyes with me again. "I suppose that could count as a *touché*. Not technically, of course, but I'll give it to you. Ask your question."

"Diamond was shot outside the Greyhound bus depot. How'd you come to be there—were you following him?"

"In a way," he said, still minding his own business on the other side of the desk. "I wasn't engaged in a mere follow, however. I was stalking him."

"Stalking him?"

He yelled, "A question!" then effortlessly put the blade to me. Even though I managed to catch it with my rapier's hand-guard, its point whirled around the thing and put a small cut on my left wrist.

"*Touché!*" he exclaimed.

I returned fire: leaned over and madly whipped and stabbed my sword across the desk at him. He backed off. Good as he was, he didn't seem to like that approach much—either that, or he was still toying with me. "You owe me an answer, you bastard," I told him.

"Quite," he replied. "Yes, I stalked Dennis Diamond. The man had invaded my territory, wanted my nymph, and threatened my life." He paused, then asked, "Did you ever see that movie, *The Most Dangerous Game*, Mr. Rossiter?"

"Can't say as I have."

He smiled—bent his rapier half-double, then let it spring deadly straight again. "It's about a hunter, a big-game hunter, who's bagged every imaginable type of game except one: man—the most dangerous game."

I lunged across at him—slashed like a banshee. Even caught by surprise, he parried everything I threw at him. Except one: I managed to leave a small slice across the back of his sword-hand.

Amazingly, Bennington liked it. He grinned, dabbed at the bit of blood, and said, "That's precisely it, Mr. Rossiter. *Man* is the most dangerous game. You've proved it perfectly: even cornered and totally overmatched, man is the most cunning, devious, and formidable adversary of all. He also thinks and reasons, which makes him ever more dangerous. I owe you an answer."

"Just finish your story about stalking Dennis Diamond," I said, noting that Bennington was keeping a greater distance between us now that I'd managed to tag him. "I'll keep my question in reserve in case I need it later."

"Most cunning of you," he said. "It occurred to me that I'd hunted every type of beast except man. Why it hadn't come to me sooner, I don't know. But, in that moment, I realized that Dennis Diamond was tailor-made to take me to the ultimate level, especially with *his* deadly reputation. I must say, it was quite an exhilarating revelation."

"So, you went after him."

"Not immediately," he told me. "You have to plan the hunt. More importantly, you have to relish the hunt, savor its inherent danger," he continued, a hungry look coming into his eyes like he was reliving the experience. "The kill itself is anticlimactic, Mr. Rossiter—it's the hunt that's everything."

"Sure," I agreed, hoping he'd get so carried away that I'd get an opening to stick him good.

"Yes," Bennington said, pacing back and forth a bit as he continued. "First, I used my many contacts to locate my prey. Next, I surveyed its range and habits. Last, I selected the appropriate weapon. Only then was I ready to begin the hunt." He stopped pacing and turned to face me, his eyes wide and a little crazy-wild. "And yes," he explained, "I was well aware of the ultimate fate of that movie's protagonist: that hunter ended up being bagged by his own quarry. But that was the delicious part," he fairly shouted. "The extreme jeopardy! The thrill of it all. I hadn't felt so alive in years!"

"Cut to the chase," I told him. "What happened?"

"You've just used your question," he told me, very calmly.

Then he switched back to his previous state of agitation. "Did you know that Mr. Diamond was Jewish, Mr. Rossiter? There was a menorah on his buffet. A prayer shawl, too. And laying right beside them? Two pistols, a blackjack, and a large stiletto. A religious gangster. I don't know if he practiced his faith or not, but I found the mix quite exciting."

"Get on with it, Bennington," I said, edging out past the desk a bit. When he didn't react to my movement, I added, "I don't give a damn about the hunt. I want to know about the kill."

He seemed disappointed. "All right. Have it your way," he said. "I tracked my prey all around town—even to the Pampas Grill where you lunched with him. At length, I felt ready to make the kill. Imagine my surprise when Diamond parked behind the Greyhound bus depot, and stood watching while Dolores and Miss Jenkins got out of a Plymouth coupe and went into the bus station." He gave me a sharp nod, said, "How about that? He was stalking Dolores while I was stalking him. Anyway, Diamond started forward, but didn't get very far. I had the .453 at the ready and, the streets being mostly deserted, felt quite at ease. I called his name to make it more sporting and, when he turned and reached for his pistol, I squeezed off the kill shot. When he went down, I wanted a trophy. I put the rifle back in my car, ran to his side, and began to cut off his little finger with my pocketknife. He lifted his head—I was shocked that he was still alive. But not for long. He managed just one word, 'Trixie,' then gasped his last."

"Trixie?" I asked. "His last word was Trixie?"

"Yes," said Bennington, not even calling the question on me—he was too wrapped up in the excitement of his story. "Curious, don't you think?" he continued. "I wrapped the

215

finger in my handkerchief and put it in my pocket. Then I hurried into the bus terminal to retrieve my nymph only to see her being led away from the locker area by your Miss Jenkins and a heavy-set fellow."

"That'd be my man, Heine."

"One of yours? I assumed he was a police detective," he said. "Well, I didn't know what Dolores had done, but I thought I'd lost her forever. Imagine my surprise when I caught the two ladies in my study a few hours later trying to steal the photos I took of your comely partner."

He grinned and flexed his rapier again. "You know the rest of the story," he told me. "And here we are now, engaged in our fencing match. You owe me at least another *touché. En garde!*"

He lunged. I jumped back, took the crystal ashtray on the desk and threw it at him. I missed.

Bennington held his position. "Your style's very ugly, Mr. Rossiter. You know, there is a much more pleasant way to end our duel."

"Yeah?"

"Of course. What I really, truly want is to have you come and work for me."

"You've got to be kidding."

"We would be wonderful together. You and Miss Jenkins both. I'm sure she's learned her lesson, now. Money's no object," he said, smiling his warmest smile. "All I need is your assent. Just the slightest submission to my will."

"I work alone."

"Come, come, Mr. Rossiter. Everybody's controlled by somebody. I'd be a most gracious and generous taskmaster. So would many of my highly placed friends. We'd have many interesting and lucrative assignments for you."

"Go to hell."

"So be it!" He threw back his robe and placed his left hand on his hip again. "Perhaps when I've made a proper pincushion of you, you'll rethink my offer." Then he reached out ever so gracefully and nicked me in the elbow, followed by a prick in the forearm. He'd just been playing with me up to this point—he was so good with the rapier he could put it to me anytime he wanted.

I slashed and whipped and windmilled my sword at him. He didn't like it, but kept coming, and backed me into the corner beside the desk.

Corners I understood from my boxing days: you didn't want to get trapped in them unless you had the power to punch your way out. But I had no power at the moment. Not against *his* flashing, dancing blade.

I needed something to even the odds. I ducked a thrust, reached way over and grabbed his oak desk chair. It had good rollers and pulled between us easily. I shoved it forward and it caught him in the shin. Guess it smarted because it backed him up. I went on the attack—kept pushing the chair forward and cutting at him with all I had—figured it would be worth taking a bad stick from him if I could deliver a killing stab of my own.

Bennington's smug expression changed as I drove him into the center of the room. A little fear showed on his face for the first time as he saw that I wasn't staying a chump. Then he smiled, set himself as I tried bashing him again with the chair, stuck me in the hand, and kicked it out of my grasp. The chair rolled a good ten feet away and fell over.

To hell with it! I charged—faked high, but went low—got in under his outstretched arm and landed a hard left hook to his chin with the hilt of my sword. Damned if he didn't spin all the way around with the force of my blow and catch me cold on the flip-side, smack in the noggin with the hilt of his own rapier. My blade went flying, and I went down like a sack of spuds.

Bennington stood over me. Feeling at his chin with his free hand, he smirked and said, "Not bad. Very resourceful. Ready to join my employ, now, Mr. Rossiter?"

I struggled up to a sitting position. "Not on your life."

He stepped back—assumed the fencer's pose again, the tip of his rapier pointed right between my eyes. "A little more persuasion is in order," he told me.

The door to the study suddenly flew open. Bennington and I turned to look at the same time. Standing in the doorway, her legs set wide apart and her dress all rumpled, was Miss Jenkins with a big, black bullwhip in her hand. In the split-second it took to note her crazed eyes and expression, she cracked the whip. It snaked out at Bennington, but was a bit off the mark. Instead of hitting the target with a vicious snap, it smacked into floor about a foot away from him—which wasn't surprising, considering I'd never known Miss Jenkins to use a bullwhip before.

But it was enough to distract Bennington. Jumping to my feet, I delivered a thundering uppercut just as he turned back to face me, then put the deadwood to him with a chopping left. He went down hard and stayed down.

"Well, you're about a day late and a dollar short," I told Miss Jenkins, retrieving my .45 from the sash at Bennington's waist.

She stalked forward, re-coiling her bullwhip, and glared down at Bennington, then at me. "Well, I was locked in a cage, for God's sake. What do you expect?"

"How'd you get out?" I asked her.

"Donny and Martin," she said, giving Bennington a kick in the ribs.

"Good for them," I said. "Say, just how'd you come to be in this fix?"

"This dirty rat locked me up."

Bennington lifted his head and sneered at Miss Jenkins. "You were very naughty," he told her, wiping at his bloody nose.

"You had no right to take those pictures!" she yelled at him. "I want them back!"

I pulled her racy photos from my pocket, and held them up for her to see. "*These* pictures?"

Her face went ashen. "Gimme those!" She snatched the photos out of my hand. Then, for once, she was simply speechless—just stared back and forth between the dirty photographs and me, and grew redder and redder in the face. She'd have grown absolutely crimson if she realized I still had one in my inside pocket.

"Hold down the fort a minute, will you, doll?" I asked her. "I've got to get something downstairs."

"Like what?"

I gave her the rundown on Diamond's missing finger. Then I took off to get it. I noticed that she booted Bennington one more time as I went out the door.

I got down to the bar in short order, and went straight back to the bartender.

I didn't see the jar in question on the counter.

"That jar," I told him. "Where is it?"

"The one with the finger in it?" he asked.

"Yeah. Where the hell is it?"

"Damned if I know," he told me. "The butler took it."

Epilogue

I NEVER DID FIND OUT WHO KILLED TRIXIE. The most obvious suspect, Chuck, insisted he was innocent. He demanded a polygraph test and passed it. The prints on the murder weapon turned out to be Royce Bennington's, which made sense, as he owned the curved blade in question. There were some other prints, but they were all smudged and no good.

The cops had nothing on Donny. I had nothing on Adrian. Or anybody else. As to Dennis Diamond, well, aside from his cryptic dying word to Bennington, "Trixie," nothing further turned up that even remotely incriminated him, except for Dolores who kept insisting he was the killer.

Some cases just never get solved, I kept telling myself. It stinks, but all you can do is your best—you can let it eat at you or move on.

We never found Dennis Diamond's missing finger. Maybe the butler flushed it down the toilet or fed it to a dog. My accusations against Royce Bennington were in the same state: basically moot. Without any concrete evidence—the squashed bullet was no good for ballistics, and the rifle was never found—my insistence that Bennington had murdered Diamond ended up being just my word against his.

Easy to guess the outcome of that contest. Between all the high-connected bigwigs he knew, and all the dirty little secrets he held, Bennington got off with just a slap on the wrist. Oh, Lt. Baker and I did get a single charge to stick— the false imprisonment of Miss Jenkins and Dolores—but it never even got to trial. Haggerty, of all people, helped plea bargain it down to a fine and probation. To boot, Bennington threatened to charge Miss Jenkins and Dolores with burglary if we pursued anything further. So, old Royce got a walk.

Then, Rollo Mudd's check bounced. I was wise enough not to call him a piker. He'd just lost his best boy, and I didn't think it would be too safe to rub salt in the wound. So, I was out his dough as well as the green I'd counted on from Lorna Horowitz's hubby. Luckily, Abe Horowitz never sued me. Maybe because Lorna convinced him to take her back.

Heine took it hard. He got into fights, drank like a fish, and the quality of his work, even his pool-sharking, went all to hell. In simple terms, my best pal, the toughest nut I ever knew, had been ruined by a conniving dame. I ended up telling him to take some time off and get himself back together. He said he would, but didn't know how long it would take. The way he said it—all subdued and almost emotionless— made me wonder if he'd *ever* be back.

I had to bring Manny Velcker on board full time to help handle Heine's load. Miss Jenkins was a pip—pitched in wherever she could—and worked long hours with Velcker. In fact, she spent so much time out in the field I virtually didn't see her for about four weeks.

I really started to miss her. Missed those days when we'd throw jokes and jibes back and forth in the office. Even missed the days that she'd get pissed and go storming out the door. Seeing her desk empty most of the time left me feeling at real loose ends.

I needed to have a heart-to-heart with her. I was happy we'd have a chance for a nice chat at the party Donny and Martin were hosting to celebrate their getting back together.

I dressed in my best blue suit—the pinstriped one that Miss Jenkins so favored. I put fresh pomade in my pompadour, and a couple extra splashes of Lilac Vegetal on my kisser. I gave my oxfords a final buff, then blew out for the Garden of Allah just as the sun was setting.

There were tons of folks in the club when I entered through the French doors. I was surprised to see how full the place was. Even so, I spotted Miss Jenkins, past the bar, on the far side of the room. She looked like a million bucks—wore a dress I hadn't seen before: a stylish, peacock-blue thing that was ultra-fetching and sexy. She was talking with Adrian, who wore his own hot number, a low-cut, cream-colored dress with matching gloves and high-heels.

I took off my coat and fedora, and smoothed back my hair. I started over to say hello to Miss Jenkins, but got waylaid by Donny and Martin.

"Jake," said Donny, "I'm so glad you could make it."

"Likewise," Martin told me. They were dressed alike in light-colored sports coats and dark, turtleneck sweaters. "Let me get you a drink."

"Thanks. Make it a Cutty, neat," I told him.

"We can't thank you enough, Jake," said Donny, as Martin went to get my hooch. "I don't know what we'd of done without you."

"I didn't do all that much," I said.

"Oh, yes you did," he said, shaking my hand. "Anyway,

we've been back together for just over a month. We're not seeing other people anymore," he told me, "only each other. Consider us monogamous."

"I'm happy for you," I said, glancing over and noting that Miss Jenkins was still talking to Adrian on the other side of the room.

"Thanks," Donny said. He looked sad for a moment. "You know how love is, Jake—it can be hard."

Just then, Martin returned with my Scotch and a belt for himself. As I took my glass from him, somebody across the way yelled for Donny to come over.

"Sorry," Donny told me, "got to see to my guests. I'll talk to you later."

I watched him go, then turned to Martin. "Congratulations, Martin," I said. "Donny told me how well you two have been getting along."

"Thanks," he said, clinking his glass into mine. "There's one big thing we've learned," he told me. "If you're lucky enough to find a person you truly love, you have to tell them so and keep telling them so. You can't take them for granted, or you could end up losing each other like we almost did."

"That's the truth," I said. "Well, I think I'll go mingle. See you in a bit."

"Anything you need," said Martin, as I headed off toward Miss Jenkins again, "you just holler."

Pushing through the crowd, I saw Manny Velcker up ahead. He veered away from me and went toward the bar, but I caught up with him.

Snazzy as ever in a two-tone, short jacket with a red shirt, its wide collar spread out over the jacket's lapels, he said, "Oh, hey Jake," when I put out my hand.

"Hiya, Manny," I told him. He gave me briefest of hand-shakes. "Everything O.K.? How's the Hoffman case going for you and Miss Jenkins?"

"Hunky-dory," he said, barely making eye contact with me. "Well, I gotta hit the head, Jake. I'll talk to you later." With that, he took off past me toward the restrooms up by the coat check.

I watched as he split, feeling like I'd just gotten the brush-off, when a heavy hand clamped onto the back of my shoulder. "Jake," said a familiar voice. It was my bear of an attorney, Haggerty. Wearing one of his zillion-dollar suits, his tie loose around the neck, he took the big stogie out of his mouth, and said, rather quietly, "You doing all right?"

"Yeah," I told him. "Any reason I shouldn't?"

"No, no. None at all." He was silent for a second—looked uncomfortable, then said, "I just hope you don't blame me for anything."

"People blame their lawyers for *everything*," I told him. "What's new about that?"

He managed a weak smile. "You know what I mean."

"You were just doing your job, Haggerty. I understand. If you can live with yourself, that's good enough for me."

"Jake." He acted a little hurt. "Look, I—"

"I'll catch you later," I told him. "Don't worry, I want to snag Miss Jenkins before she gets off somewhere else."

He started to open his mouth again, but I was already on my way to my partner's side. Miss Jenkins and Adrian were so engaged in conversation that neither of them noticed me as I approached.

"I just *love* this fabric," Miss Jenkins told Adrian, running her fingers along the material at the arm of his dress.

"Dolores made it for me," said Adrian, smiling at the

compliment, as he pushed a stray lock of his long, blonde wig back into place.

"Yes, I know. She made this one for me. She's going to make all my dresses from now on."

"Don't look now," Adrian told Miss Jenkins as I walked up, "but here comes that hunky partner of yours."

"Hi, doll," I said, as I reached Miss Jenkins's side. "You're looking swell."

"What about me?" Adrian asked. He put his hands on his hips and batted his eyelashes. "You like?"

"Yeah, very chic." I took Miss Jenkins by the arm. "Let's talk," I said, moving her away from Adrian where we could have a little privacy.

"That was rude," Miss Jenkins told me when we'd gotten off by ourselves.

"Sorry, I just wanted to have a moment alone with you."

"O.K. We're alone. What is it?"

I hesitated. Funny, now that I had her alone, I didn't know quite what to say.

"Well?" she asked. "Something up?"

I studied her for a moment. Loved the way her strawberry-blonde locks contrasted with her new, peacock-blue dress—also liked the extra-leggy look that her high-heels gave her petite and trim figure.

"Well?" she repeated, starting to impatiently tap one pointy-toed high-heel. "Cat got your tongue? This isn't like you at all."

I moved closer to her. "You know, we've been through a lot together, doll."

She gave me a queer look. "Yes?"

I opened my mouth again, but nothing came out. I just stood there staring into her bright, green-blue eyes like some schoolboy on his first date. I knew I was going to say something to her—something genuine, not flippant for a change—but I sure had no clue that I was going to end up telling Miss Jenkins what I told her.

Maybe it was just the happy spirit of Donny and Martin's little celebration. Maybe it was waking up in her bed that one morning, and how nice it might be to do it for real, maybe every morning. Maybe it was all the times that I'd feared for her safety, had actually felt like a piece of me was in danger. Or maybe it was just me getting a little older and wiser, finally recognizing someone I could really trust and realizing what a precious thing that was. Or maybe I was just afraid that I'd slide all the way down the tubes to some permanent address on queer street if I didn't change my ways…

Whatever it was, I finally got my lips into gear, and blurted, "Miss Jenkins, I think I love you."

"What?" She looked as shocked as I was by what I said.

"No. Strike that," I told her, warming to the subject now that I'd spit it out. "There's no doubt whatsoever." I took her right hand in mine and gave it a healthy squeeze. "I love you, Barbara."

"Well…" She looked like she was about to cry. "You're about a day late and a dollar short."

"What do you mean?"

"We were going to announce it tonight at the party." She pulled her hand away.

"Announce what?"

"Didn't you notice?" she asked, holding up her left hand. A big, gold, diamond ring—its sparkling stone at least a full carat—adorned her ring-finger. "Manny just asked me to marry him, and I accepted. We're engaged."

226

Again, my deepest thanks to Waverly Fitzgerald, without whom this book and the two before it would have been incomplete.

The author also owes more than he can say to the UglyBoys: the incomparable publishing and editorial duo aka Tom Fassbender & Jim Pascoe.

Special thanks to Paul Dorpat, author and historian, whose "Seattle Now and Then" series first clued me to the existence of Seattle's historic gay cabaret, the Garden of Allah.

Also, my gratitude to all my friends who helped and put up with me while writing this book.

And last, but not least, my love and affection to my wife, Stephanie, who never quite succeeded in getting me to clean my office.

THE JAKE ROSSITER & MISS JENKINS SERIES
CONTINUES IN

Nowhere Town

Preview

Whoever it was took another shot at me.

In the pitch dark and driving rain, I saw the shooter's large form briefly outlined in the pistol's muzzle flash. The bullet hit the pavement and ricocheted up, grazing my right calf—seared like a branding iron.

I ducked into the alley and ran for all I was worth, slipping on the wet bricks, knocking over several garbage cans—still couldn't see who was after me, didn't know why he wanted to punch my ticket. All I knew was that I was alone, hurt and unarmed, and could hear footsteps catching up to me.

What the fuck had happened two months ago to put me in this fix?

No time to think: he was shooting again—maybe firing blindly, but any of the three slugs that tore my direction could have had my name on it.

The police cruiser I'd stolen was parked near the mouth of the narrow, block-long alley. Less than half a block to go, I ran into the twilight that drifted onto the bricks from the single working streetlamp at the alley's end—knew I'd just become a better target.

I ducked, I juked, I bobbed and weaved—somehow, the next two bullets missed me. I skinned my knuckles jerking open the cruiser's door. Got it revved and fishtailed a quarter block before I even thought to pull the door closed. Caught a glimpse in the rear-view of the big man in the overcoat and slouch-hat blasting away at me again.

Flash-flash-flash-pop-pop-pop!

The cruiser's back window shattered, glass flying all the way to me at the wheel, cutting the back of my head and bouncing off the dashboard like so many pissed-off bees.

Third & Cherry, I pulled over and assessed the damage. Nothing my handkerchief wouldn't staunch tied tight around my aching calf; nothing that wouldn't clot soon on the back of my noggin; nothing the cops' grease-monkey's couldn't fix if they ever got their cruiser back—and nothing, but nothing I wouldn't do to find out the the score, then settle somebody's fucking hash.

Right now, though, I needed a place to hole up. Cops had a dragnet out on me; my own damned operatives couldn't be trusted; and I generally felt like I was coming off a two-week bender.

Downtown's tall buildings raced by as I lead-footed it east, up the black and slippery slopes toward the south end of Capitol Hill and the only haven I could think of at the moment: Sugar Joe's Gym in Negro Town.